FRIGHTMARES

A CREEPY COLLECTION
OF SCARY STORIES

BY MICHAEL DAHL

ILLUSTRATED BY XAVIER BONET

P9-DDG-019

STONE ARCH BOOKS
a capstone imprint

TABLE OF CONTENTS

SECTION 1: INSIDE THE HOUSE

SECTION 2: AROUND THE CORNER

SECTION 3: OUT OF YOUR MIND

Dear Reader,

I LIVE IN A HAUNTED HOUSE.

Not everyone believes me, but I've seen the ghost. Her name is Helen. One night I stood at the end of my hallway and saw Helen glide into my bedroom.

That's the only word for it. *Glide.*

I slept on the couch that night.

The previous owners told me Helen's name. They did not tell me what she looked like. I found that out for myself.

It seems we all find out what scares us when we are alone.

Now it's your turn to be alone. Alone with this book. Just you and the pages and the stories. You'll find out what scares the people in these stories.

At the same time, you might also find out what scares you . . .

Michael Dahl

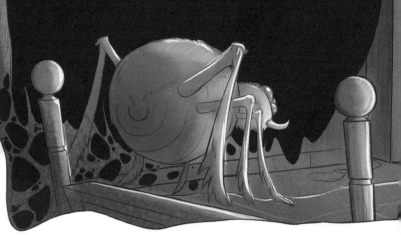

SECTION 1

INSIDE THE HOUSE

THE STRANGER ON THE STAIRS

Six-year-old Brandon Spode hated climbing the stairs at night.

"Time for bed, Brandon," said his mother. "Up to your room."

"I don't want to," Brandon moaned.

"Don't tell me it's the man again," said Mrs. Spode.

"He's sitting up there," said Brandon.

Mrs. Spode stood at the bottom of the stairs, her hands on her hips, and looked up. "There's nothing there," she said.

Mrs. Spode had braces on her legs, so she never climbed the stairs herself. Her bedroom was on the main floor.

Brandon pointed. "He's right there."

"That's a shadow," said Mrs. Spode. "The light in the hallway makes a shadow. You know what a shadow is, don't you?"

Brandon nodded. He knew what a shadow was. But he also knew that the man on the stairs wasn't made by light and shadows.

The man sat there every night on the top step. His skin was the color of a red crayon that had melted on the sidewalk. His eyebrows were thick and bushy. He had a wide grin that stretched his face tight, like the skin of a balloon. Three reddish bumps grew on his forehead.

"I don't want to go to bed," said Brandon.

Mrs. Spode was tired of having the same argument every night. "This time I'll stand right here and watch you go up the stairs," she said. "All right?"

Brandon didn't move.

"It's getting late, young man," his mother said.

Slowly, Brandon took the first step.

The man on the stairs never moved. When Brandon had first seen him, he thought the man was a statue. But when he passed him,

Brandon could hear breathing. Then one night, he saw the man blink.

"Hurry up, Brandon. I can't stand here all night, can I?" said Mrs. Spode.

The boy approached the figure at the top step.

"Keep going," said his mother.

Brandon heard breathing. He could see white teeth gleaming in the stretched-out grin.

The boy shut his eyes. He kept climbing. He put his right hand against the wall to guide him. Brandon stumbled a bit when his stocking feet reached the hallway. He was at the top. He opened his eyes and looked down at his mother.

"See, I told you," said Mrs. Spode, crossing her arms. "There's no man sitting on the stairs, now is there?"

"No," Brandon said softly.

"Then get to bed," ordered his mother. The woman turned and saw a man standing behind her. A man with a red face, bumps on his forehead, and a wide, stretchy smile.

Upstairs, Brandon heard a scream and then a thud as his mother fainted and hit the floor.

KNOCK,
KNOCK

Noah and his older brother, Sky, both folded their arms and stared at their parents across the dinner table.

"I don't believe it," said Sky.

"You only have to share a bedroom for a week," their mother explained patiently.

"I want my own room," Sky said, pouting.

"As soon as we are finished painting," said their father, "you will each have your own room."

"This place is creepy," said Noah.

Their mother sighed and said, "It's not creepy. There's so much sunshine and fresh air."

It's got sunshine, thought Noah, *because there aren't any trees.*

Their new home had been a boarding house for loggers a hundred years ago. It sat in the middle of boggy fields. The trees for miles around had all been cut down. There was nothing around but whispering cattails and jabbering frogs. The driveway was dirt, and it didn't meet another road for at least five miles. The giant house had four porches, a front parlor with five sofas, a sauna built into the side of a hill, and more than a dozen bedrooms.

Creepy, Noah had decided.

That night, the brothers trudged angrily up to the third floor of the new house and got ready for bed. Sky rested his head on his pillow and stared over at his brother's bed. "I hope the ghosts don't keep you awake," he said, smiling.

Noah could see his brother's teeth shine in the darkness. "Quit it, Sky," he said.

"Oh, you didn't know?" said Sky. "Yeah, Dad told me this place is haunted."

"I said, quit it!"

"One of the old loggers died outside during a blizzard," Sky continued. "He went out to pee, and the door locked behind him."

"I mean it!"

"He knocked and knocked," Sky said, "but no one heard him. The wind was too loud. And in the morning, they found him dead on the doorstep, frozen solid."

"Yeah, right." Noah rolled his eyes. He didn't believe his brother at all.

"His hand was frozen in midair," Sky continued. "Like he was trying to knock."

"I'm telling Dad in the morning if you don't stop," said Noah.

"Morning is a long way away," said Sky. Then he snapped off the bedside lamp they both shared and turned over to sleep. "Well, good night, bro."

Noah didn't say anything. He gripped the covers and listened to the wind as it rumbled across the ancient roof.

It's June. There's no chance of a blizzard, Noah thought.

He grew tired, and he finally drifted off to sleep.

But in the middle of the night, he woke up with a start. What was that noise? *Just the wind again,* Noah told himself.

Why did Sky have to tell me that stupid story about the dead logger anyway? Noah wondered. *Even if there was a ghost, what would he be doing up here on the third floor? He'd still be outside, knocking on the door where he died . . . right?* He took a deep breath and leaned back on his pillow.

Tomorrow night, Noah decided, *I'll tell Sky a spooky story. A story about a ghost with burning eyes. Let him try to sleep peacefully tonight, though —*

Knock, knock.

Noah slowly peered over his covers.

Knock, knock.

The sound came from their half-open door.

"Cut it out, Sky," said Noah. He glanced over toward his brother. It was hard to see in the dim moonlight, but it looked like Sky's bed was empty.

Knock, knock.

Noah stared at the door. A shadow stood in the hallway. Tall and heavy, like their father. It didn't move.

"Dad?" croaked Noah. His tongue and lips felt dry.

The shadow grew darker, then faded away. Noah blinked a few times. *My eyes are tired,* he thought. *That's all.*

.y," he called weakly.

He heard another sound. Not exactly a knock, but . . . more like a bump. And it came from beyond Sky's bed. It came from their closet.

Noah was angry now. This was too much.

He threw off his blankets and jumped up out of bed. He stomped over to the closet and yanked open the door. "Ha, ha! Funny, Sky!" he said.

On the floor of the closet sat his brother. Sky was hunched up, holding his knees to his chest and staring up at Noah in terror. His mouth opened a few times, but nothing came out. Then Sky whispered, "Don't — don't let it in."

Noah felt something grip his shoulder. A cold, hard hand.

COLD SEAT

It was the thing Jake hated more than anything else about winter: a cold toilet seat.

And tonight, that was exactly what he had to look forward to.

His parents and older sister were at a family get-together for New Year's Eve. Jake had refused to go. There had been a big fight, and he ended up staying home alone. When his family drove off, Jake called his friend Phil, who was planning to have a bunch of people over. Phil didn't pick up. Jake tried a few other numbers, but no one answered.

Everyone was out having a good time.

A warm time.

Jake's dad insisted on keeping their thermostat set at 62 degrees. "It saves money," he always said.

But whenever the heat was set at 62 degrees, the toilet seat was freezing. Jake didn't care how much money it cost to keep his butt warm, but his dad never backed down. And if Jake turned up the heat while his parents were at the party, he knew they'd find out somehow. They always did.

And now Jake had to use the bathroom.

He had been watching the late news on TV, watching all the parties that were happening around the world. Happening without him.

A reporter came on and aired a story about local break-ins. Most houses were empty that evening because their owners were out celebrating all night. It was prime time for burglars and thieves. Some of them could be dangerous.

Just what I need to hear, thought Jake as he pressed the remote.

No matter how many times he switched channels, though, he couldn't switch off the call of nature. And the longer he waited, the colder it would be. That toilet seat would be good and frosty. Especially since he was home alone, and there was no one around to use it before him and warm it up.

Jake trudged down the dark hallway to the bathroom. He prepared himself for the chill against his tender skin. Sitting on the cool stool always reminded him of jumping into a pool full of cold water. Or falling into a snow bank.

Grow up, he thought as he entered the dark bathroom. He didn't flick on the light switch, because he never did. The little moon-shaped nightlight over the sink was usually enough to see by.

Gently, Jake lowered himself onto the seat.

He gasped.

And not because of the cold.

The seat was warm. Nice and warm. As if someone had just been sitting there.

The shower curtain rustled.

THE
LAVA
GAME

Cory was trying to be a good brother. He was trying very hard. But this was too much.

His little brother, Kyle, and his friends were upstairs yelling in the living room.

"Stay off the floor!"

"Quick! Jump on the sofa!"

"No, don't go that way. You'll fall in the lava and die!"

Cory rolled his eyes. *Kids still play that dumb game?* he thought.

The point of the Lava Game was to pretend that the carpet or floor was really hot, molten lava. If you took one wrong step, you could die a painful, fiery death. The living room was the best place to play the Lava Game. It had lots of sofas and chairs and tables to step on, crawl over, climb up, and leap to over the lava.

Cory was trying to concentrate on his video game downstairs in the basement, but he could still hear their annoying little voices through the floorboards.

Why had he even volunteered to babysit Kyle and his friends? Kyle was eight — old enough to be on his own. He didn't need a thirteen-year-old telling him what to do. But now Cory was getting annoyed. He was busy fighting off a shipload of alien soldiers, and Kyle and his friends were being too loud.

Cory ran upstairs.

"Keep it down, you little creeps!" Cory shouted. He planted himself in the archway to the living room. Kyle and his friends froze. They each stood on a different piece of furniture.

"We're trying to survive here," said Kyle, waving his arms.

"Yeah, dude," echoed one of his friends. Cory thought the kid's name was Bree or Ree or something. "We can't die!" the kid said.

"I can't believe you guys still play that game," Cory said with a smirk.

"It's not a game," said Kyle. "It's life or death!"

"I thought you'd have outgrown playing Lava by now," said Cory.

Kyle and his friends looked at one another. "What's Lava?" asked Bree or Ree.

Cory had taken a few steps into the living room. It was too late.

"It's quicksand!" yelled Kyle. "The floor is quicksand."

Cory didn't realize what was happening until he had sunk up to his knees in the thick green carpet. He could feel something warm and mushy. It felt like half mud, half pudding.

Kyle and his friends screamed. "Get out! Get out!"

Cory was so startled he couldn't speak. He flailed his arms, looking for something solid to grab on to. Now he was up to his chest. He was too far from any furniture.

"Kyle," he cried. "Help!"

Kyle looked around, helpless. Then he pulled up one of the cushions from the sofa he stood on. He threw it toward his brother who grabbed it with both hands. Cory held onto it but the cushion sank into the carpet like a cracker in hot soup.

The thick carpet was up to Cory's chin.

"What do we do?!" yelled Bree or Ree.

"I can't reach him!" screamed Kyle.

"Stay off the floor! You'll fall in and sink too!" cried another friend.

"Cory!"

Cory sank out of sight, his hands grasping at the air.

The carpet closed over him. It was smooth and still, as if nothing had ever been there. A part of the carpet bunched up suddenly into a small bump, a bubble. Then it was gone.

"My mother's going to kill me," moaned Kyle.

DON'T LET THE BEDBUG BITE

"Bedbug! Bedbug!" shouted the little boy.

"That's just Norman's way of saying he doesn't want to go to bed," his mother, Mrs. Brocken, explained to the babysitter.

"Bedbug!" Norman said again.

"He's been saying that ever since the other night," said Mrs. Brocken. "My husband told him, 'Good night, sleep tight, don't let the bedbugs bite.'"

"Bite! Bite!" said Norman.

"You can ignore him, Cleo," Mrs. Brocken said. "Put him to bed right at eight o'clock."

Norman sobbed.

Cleo Henderson babysat for all the families in the neighborhood. This was the first time she had been hired by the Brockens.

Norman was cute. He had curly red hair and bright-blue eyes. But now his eyes were filling up with tears. Baby tears. And Cleo hated baby tears. She felt helpless whenever she saw them. She knew that being the babysitter meant that she was in charge. But baby tears always got to her.

"Maybe we can stay up and read a story if he has trouble sleeping?" asked Cleo, looking at Mrs. Brocken.

"Bedtime is eight o'clock," said Mrs. Brocken firmly. She stepped into her fancy shoes and checked her hair in the hallway mirror. Then Mr. Brocken came down the stairs. He was wearing a nice suit and tie.

Mr. Brocken looked at his crying child. "Don't tell me," he said. "Bedbugs?"

"I don't know why you ever said that to him," said Mrs. Brocken.

"Everybody says it," snapped Mr. Brocken. "It doesn't mean anything."

"Bedbug! Bedbug!" yelled the red-faced Norman.

"Does he think there are real bugs in his bed?" asked Cleo. She could understand

Norman's terror if he had seen an actual bug in his bed. Cleo hated bugs, too. She hated all creepy-crawly things.

"Who knows what's going on in his little brain," Mrs. Brocken said, picking up her purse.

"Bite! Bite!" screamed Norman.

Mr. Brocken threw up his arms. "That's enough, Norman!" he shouted.

Both Cleo and Norman were surprised. Norman even stopped crying.

"I'm going up there right now to prove that there are no — I repeat *no* — bedbugs!" Mr. Brocken continued. "And then you are going to bed!" He angrily marched up the stairs, and Cleo heard a door bang shut.

The house was totally quiet. Then Mrs. Brocken said, "See, Norman? See what you've done? You made your daddy really mad and ruined —"

Suddenly, a terrible scream came from upstairs. It came from Norman's room.

Mrs. Brocken raced upstairs, followed closely by Cleo, who held onto Norman's hand.

When they opened the bedroom door, they found Mr. Brocken lying quietly on Norman's bed. He looked like he was fast asleep.

"What are you doing?" asked Mrs. Brocken. "Why did you scream?"

Mr. Brocken didn't answer. He didn't move.

But the pillow under his head moved. A hairy black arm, about seven feet long, crept out from under the pillow. Then a second arm reached out from the other side.

Two see-through wings, like giant tennis rackets, sprung up on either side of the mattress. The legs of the bed began to shake. A loud hum filled the air.

Cleo couldn't look away from the horrible scene. Mrs. Brocken screamed. The giant bug was shaking so much now that Mr. Brocken's shoes came off his feet and slid across the bug's smooth, inky shell and down to the bedroom floor.

Then the wings flapped. The bedbug scurried over to the open bedroom window, put its long front feelers on the sill, and leaped into the air. The awful creature flew around the Brockens' backyard. Mr. Brocken still lay quietly, as if glued to the bug's back. With a loud buzz, the bug flew above the roof and was lost in the starry night sky.

"Bedbug! Bedbug!" said Norman.

Cleo hugged the little boy. He squirmed in her arms and pointed, but not at the window this time. He pointed toward a dark corner of the bedroom. Cleo saw five or six large white shapes, as round as basketballs, nestled in the corner.

They were eggs. And their shells were starting to crack.

THE BACK
OF THE
CLOSET

I wake up. It's very dark. Everyone should be in bed by now, but I can hear footsteps. They're by the closet.

Creeeeeak!

I can see the closet door opening. I'm too startled to speak. Am I dreaming? I must be dreaming, because now I see a skinny, hairless hand.

The hand opens its fingers as it reaches.

The hand pulls the cord hanging from the closet ceiling, and the light snaps on.

It's so bright!

The hand definitely belongs to one of the small humans that live in this house. None of them have seen me hiding in this closet. They don't realize that I've been here a very long time. Ever since the house was built.

No one has ever bothered to look at the very back of this closet. Lucky for me. It's in the basement of the house, and hardly any of the humans come to this particular corner. The shadows here are quite comfy.

I hope the young human doesn't see me hiding here behind these boxes. What is it looking for anyway? There's nothing in here but old, broken things.

Ah, it's reaching for an old toy. Lots of toys were left here by another family. The small human must be looking for something to do.

I decide I don't want the small human coming here to my home, so I make a noise, reach out, and spook it. And now, I'm sure it'll stay away.

Forever.

HAIKUKU

The minute arrives.

Door opens — I run! I scream!

The clock pulls me back.

DON'T MAKE A WISH

Nina stood up and faced her giant chocolate birthday cake.

"Make a wish! Make a wish!" her friends shouted. They crowded around the table to get a good look at the birthday girl.

Nina's mom and dad stood nearby, smiling, presents in their arms.

"Make a wish, honey," said her mom.

Nina thought hard. Wishes were serious. She bent toward the nine candles and blew.

"Yeah!" everyone shouted. The candles went out.

But a breeze kept blowing. A strong breeze. It blew across the table, fluttering napkins and shoving aside balloons. Party hats went flying. Birthday presents tumbled onto the floor. The wind whistled louder and louder.

Nina didn't move. She stood still, confetti and streamers swirling around her. "It's coming true," she said.

Nina's mom fought against the wind to reach her side. "What are you talking about?" she yelled. "What did you wish for?"

"I wished Great-Aunt Sally could come to my birthday party," Nina said.

"No, honey," said her mom. "Your Great-Aunt Sally died last week. Don't you remember?"

The doorbell rang.

"Someone's at the door!" yelled a kid.

Nina's parents frowned. Was it a late party guest?

Dad marched toward the door.

The wind grew stronger. It rushed against the huge birthday cake.

"No one's out here," Nina's dad called out.

Frosting slid down the sides of the cake. The candles flew into the air. The top of the cake exploded, pushed up from inside. Up rose a round white skull, dripping with chocolate. It turned to face Nina.

"Happy birthday, dear," said the skull. "I didn't think I'd make it."

SECTION 2

AROUND THE CORNER

MEET THE PARENTS

Matt Rooney sat on the sofa in the living room. He stared across the room at his favorite photo on the wall. In it, he and his parents were each holding a pair of skis. All three of them were smiling at the camera. A snowy mountain sat in the background. They had been so happy on that trip.

Tonight was different. No one was happy. And Matt was afraid. He kept looking away from his parents as they spoke to him from across the coffee table.

"Before your real parents get here, there's something you should know," said his father.

"You're going to scare him," Mrs. Rooney whispered to her husband.

"I heard that!" said Matt. "What do you mean, 'scare' me?"

Mr. Rooney cleared his throat and started over. "As I said, uh, before your real parents get here —"

"But *you're* my real parents!" shouted Matt. "I don't care that I'm adopted!"

Matt's mom sighed, her eyes watery and tired. She leaned on her husband.

"Your *natural* parents, I mean," his dad said.

"I don't want to go with them," cried Matt.

Matt's mom sat down next to him on the sofa. "You don't *have* to do anything, Mattie," she replied. "But they wrote and asked to see you, so —"

"Well, I don't want to see them," said Matt. "And you still didn't tell me what was going to scare me."

His dad looked quickly at his mother. "Well, sometimes families have problems," he said.

"Your natural mother and father had to go away for a time," added his mom. "They had no choice. And they needed someone to take care of their special baby."

"Special?" Matt asked. "Is something wrong with me?"

"There's absolutely nothing wrong with you," his dad said. "You know that." He sat down on the other side of Matt, putting his hand on his son's shoulder.

"You mean my back, don't you?" asked Matt. Matt had been born with his back covered in thick, bumpy skin. It didn't look pretty in the mirror, but Matt was used to it by now. It never stopped him from joining activities. He wore a T-shirt whenever he went swimming, but that was the only thing he did differently from his friends.

"No, I don't mean your back," said his father.

A *thud* shook the house, and Matt's dad stood up.

"What was that?" Matt said. He turned and looked out the living room window.

It was evening. Their house sat at the bend of a sharp curve. The street trailed off into darkness on either side. Two or three streetlights stretched overhead like dinosaur necks.

Thud! The windows rattled.

"Oh, honey," said Matt's mother as she jumped from the sofa and grabbed her husband's hands.

"It's them," said his father.

Thud!

"Them? Them who?" asked Matt. His father didn't answer. Instead, he went to the front door and opened it.

"Mom, who is Dad talking about?" Matt asked. His mother joined her husband at the door. They both stood there, holding hands, silently staring outside.

"*Now* you're scaring me," said Matt.

The *thuds* grew louder. Matt leaned over the back of the sofa and peered out the window.

A shadow stood in the middle of the street. It was blocks away, but even at that distance Matt could tell the creature was huge. The head of the thing almost touched the streetlights. A second slightly smaller shadow appeared behind it.

The two shadows moved forward on legs as thick as tree trunks.

"What . . . is that?" Matt asked weakly.

"Them," said his mother.

"Them who?" Matt cried again. He saw the two shadows reach out and hold hands. His head hurt. "You don't mean those — things — are . . . are . . ." He couldn't finish the sentence.

The shadows marched toward the house. They smashed through the bushes at the end of the driveway. They knocked branches off the tree in the front yard. Cracks appeared in the living room window with each new *thud*.

As the creatures came closer, an awful smell became stronger and stronger. *What is that terrible smell?* Matt wondered. It made him think of vomit on a pile of wet leaves.

A groan rumbled through the house like a thunderstorm.

His mom said in a tiny voice, "Mattie, honey, someone's asking to meet you."

Matt felt sick, but he managed to make it to the doorway without throwing up. The creatures were covered in long, droopy, vine-like stuff. *Is that their fur?* he wondered. They were walking lumps of grass. Matt saw bugs crawling over them.

The taller creature let out an ear-ringing roar. "MATT!!!"

Matt gulped. He grabbed for his mom's hand. Then he gulped again. Then he said, "Are . . . are you my . . . parents?"

The huge creatures began to shiver. The odor got worse. A swarm of bugs flew off the vines and buzzed into the house.

"I think they're laughing," said Matt's dad.

"What's so funny?" asked Matt.

The bigger one spoke. "No," boomed the deep voice. "Not your parents."

Matt sighed. *My parents aren't monsters after all,* he thought.

The second giant said, "We are servants. Work for your parents. Here they are."

A cry pierced the night air. Two strange figures soared over the treetops. They sailed above the streetlights and dove toward the ground. Graceful as eagles, they landed on the front lawn and walked to the front door on slender legs.

"Mattie!" said the female. "My baby!" The beautiful woman looked human except for the pale, bat-like wings on her back. She knelt and gave Matt a hug.

The man stood up straight and proud and shook hands with Matt's dad. "Thank you for taking care of him," he said. "We are sorry we haven't been here. But now we are allowed to visit your world for short periods of time."

"I hope you don't mind if we take Mattie for the weekend?" said the female.

Matt's mom smiled. "Of course not. Um, would you like some coffee?"

Matt couldn't speak. What was happening? His T-shirt felt tight on his body. His back stung and burned. Then he heard a ripping sound. He stumbled, gripping the side of the door for balance. All of a sudden he felt light as air.

The strange man smiled down at Matt. "Yes, my son," he said. "You have wings."

The two grassy creatures were ordered to gather up Matt's bedroom furniture and all his clothes and video games and soccer ball and books — because he wasn't sure what he'd need over the next few days. Far above them soared the reunited family.

Matt was still afraid, but his fear had changed. At the beginning of the evening, he had been afraid of who, or what, his parents might be.

Now, he was afraid of falling. He had never used wings before. He had never known he had them, folded under his bumpy back. As the cool air rushed past his face, though, he found his balance. He stretched out his arms, leaning into the wind. He was sure he would get the hang of it. It reminded him of skiing.

CLOSER
AND
CLOSER

As soon as Maddie saw the black bag, she knew something was wrong.

It looked like an ordinary black plastic garbage bag. The bigger size, the kind you could stuff leaves inside. But Maddie was certain this bag wasn't holding leaves.

Maddie saw it from the bus on her way to school. She was sitting in her regular seat halfway back on the right side of the bus. And she saw the bag before anyone else got on. Because her house on the east edge of town was the farthest one in the school district, she had a few extra minutes alone each morning before the bus filled up with chattering kids.

She liked staring out the window, watching the scenery . . . warehouses, abandoned shops, empty parking lots. Maddie planned to be an artist one day. Artists, she knew, were good observers. They saw things that other people missed.

The black bag was at the far end of an empty lot. Maddie noticed it right away because she looked for that lot every day. She had always liked this lot because it was covered with grass and delicate white flowers. What was a bag doing there? The bag was lying on its side. It was about a foot and a half high, with a piece of red yarn tied at one end. Maddie frowned. Someone had dumped garbage in the lot. They must have done it at night when no one was looking.

Some people are just trashy, Maddie thought.

On the bus ride back from school that day, Maddie counted each stop. She counted each kid as they left the bus. Finally, when she was the last passenger, Maddie quickly moved to the other side. She wanted to face the empty lot when they passed it again.

Something about the bag bothered her. It had bothered her all day at school. The dark shape was like a smudge on a beautiful painting of grass and flowers. The artist in

Maddie hated things that were out of place. That didn't belong.

Finally, the lot was coming into view. Maddie gasped.

Someone had moved the black bag. Maddie was sure she'd seen it at the end of the lot. Now it was in the middle of the lot.

Maddie dreamed about the bag that night. And on the bus the following morning, she waited impatiently for the overgrown lot to come into view. When they drove by, the bag had moved again. This time it was lying closer to the street.

Every day that week when Maddie looked for the bag, she saw that it had moved closer and closer to the bus.

On Friday morning, it was so much closer that Maddie got her best view of it. The bag was . . . *lumpy*. It looked like it held something heavy. Too heavy to be pushed by the wind.

So a person must have moved it, Maddie thought. *But who would move garbage around instead of just picking it up?*

That day, Maddie's classes dragged on forever. On the bus ride back home, when the other riders were gone, Maddie slipped across the aisle. She waited for the grassy lot to appear. Rain slid against the windows, making it harder to see outside. She squinted through the glass. There was the lot coming up. The bus slowed down for a red light.

Maddie shook her head. The bag was gone. The black shape had disappeared. There was nothing but wet grass and flowers. Maddie pressed her forehead against the window and gazed down as far as she could. It wasn't on the sidewalk or by the storm drain.

She leaned back against the seat and sighed. So much better. Someone else must have seen the trash and taken it away. Now Maddie's lot wasn't spoiled.

At her bus stop, Maddie picked up her backpack and climbed down the steps to the sidewalk. The clouds were breaking apart. Sunshine gleamed off nearby puddles. Maddie was careful to step back from the curb so she wouldn't get splashed.

As the bus pulled away, a fresh wind blew into Maddie's face.

Then she saw it. It had been hidden by the bus before. But now, across the street, atop the storm drain, lay the black bag with the red yarn tied at one end.

Maddie opened her mouth, but nothing came out. She took a few steps back, unable to take her eyes off the bag. Ever so slowly, the bag rolled over and inched its way toward her. She took a few more steps. The bag rolled again.

Maddie ran to her house.

She refused to look behind her. She raced to the side door and into the kitchen.

Her mother stood at the kitchen counter. "What in the world —" she began.

Maddie dashed past her. She ran down the hall, into her room. She shut the door behind her, breathing hard.

She was away from the street. Away from the wet and the gutters. Away from that horrible plastic thing.

Maddie took another deep breath, shuddering. The trash basket next to her dresser rustled. The plastic lining inside the basket crinkled. A black shiny lump rose from the basket's mouth as if it were blowing a bubble made of tar. It oozed over the side and onto the pink carpet. It stretched across the floor, longer and longer. A dark, oily cocoon. Then the cocoon curled up, coiling like a cobra, until it touched the ceiling of Maddie's room.

It was a dark serpent, ready to strike.

* * *

The next morning, Cara sat on the bus on the way to school. She was the first rider. She wondered where that girl named Maddie was. Maddie was always on the bus before her. First one on, last one off. Maybe she was sick.

Cara gazed out the dirty windows, lost in thought. The bus pulled up to a stoplight. Cara looked out at an empty lot she'd never noticed before. It was covered with grass and tiny white flowers. *It's like a pretty painting,* thought Cara. But something seemed out of place. At the far end of the lot lay something dark. Cara squinted. If only she were closer. It looked like a black plastic bag.

No, she was wrong.

There were two.

LOVE
BUG

"The average human swallows seventeen spiders while they sleep. Did you know that?" Doug asked, his eyes shining with excitement.

"Uh, no," said Laura.

"But that's spread out over a lifetime," added Doug. "Since we're only fourteen, we've lived, like, maybe a sixth of our lives. So we've probably only swallowed two or three by now."

"Good to know," Laura replied.

"It doesn't bother me, though," said Doug. "Since I'm a —"

They both finished his sentence together: "— bug person."

Doug sighed happily and continued to stare up at the moon.

Laura stared at Doug, then down at her hands in her lap. She was wearing her new sky-blue dress. She and her mother had bought it for the middle-school dance. Doug hadn't said anything about it.

Maybe, Laura thought, *if it had been decorated with beetles or centipedes or millipedes — maybe then, Doug would have noticed.*

At least he was nice. And he looked cute in his polo shirt and tie.

"Why are you letting Doug the Bug take you to the dance?" her shocked friends had all asked her earlier that week.

"Buggy Dougie is creepy," her friend Vanda had said.

"I wouldn't say creepy," her other friend Caroline had said. "But he *is* a nerd. A bug nerd. Yuck."

"A cute nerd," Laura had said quietly.

Besides, the boy she had hoped would ask her to the dance, Powell, hadn't said a word to her all week. Nothing. He hadn't showed up at the dance that night either. Neither had his friends. They probably thought it was stupid.

More likely, thought Laura, *they just didn't have the guts to ask a girl out.*

Boys were odd creatures, Laura knew. An entirely different species from girls.

At least Doug had asked her. He was nice, too. He had danced with her, not well, but he'd tried. And he'd sat next to her when they ate and talked. Mostly about bugs.

"So, what were those millipedes you talked about before?" Laura asked.

They were sitting on a bench just a block from school. Doug had offered to walk Laura home. They had decided to take a shortcut through the park. Then Laura had suggested they sit by the lake for a bit. The smooth water shone in the full moonlight like an icy skating rink. The air was warm and still.

"Yeah," Doug replied. "'Millepede' means a thousand feet. But they don't really have a thousand. They have lots of them, though. Dozens. They can even have, like, three hundred feet!"

"I never knew that," said Laura.

"Yes," said Doug, his face shining in the moonlight. "They're amazing creatures. In fact, they're my favorite. If I ever came back in another life, I'd want to come back as a millipede."

"Oh," said Laura.

"But some of them are poisonous," Doug explained. "So I'd have to be careful."

"Right."

"How about you?" Doug asked. "What would you want to come back as?"

Laura thought for a moment. No one had ever asked her that question. "Hmm, maybe a deer. Or a gazelle," she said. "Something graceful."

"Yeah, gazelles are beautiful," said Doug.

He sighed happily again, and this time he reached over and took Laura's hand. She let him. It felt nice, sitting in the moonlight with a cute boy. Just sitting and holding hands and talking. Even if they were talking about millipedes. Even if the boy was Doug the Bug.

Laura looked up at the moon and smiled.

She felt Doug's hand in hers. Then he put his other hand around her waist. And his other hand wrapped around her shoulder, and his other hand held out a flower, and his other hand brushed her hair back, and . . .

PICKLED

It was Tom's idea to take the shortcut home on the last day of school.

Gus, Raymond, and I followed him out of the school building, past the buses, past the screaming kids. He led us into the woods behind the school. It was faster than walking through the neighborhood and much cooler than taking the bus.

We had heard stories about the woods. Grown-ups said there had been a farm there years ago. A tornado had ripped through the town, across the fields, and swept up the farmer, his family, and his entire house. There was nothing left but a few lost pigs and a cow.

Trees and weeds took over the abandoned fields. No one ever moved in.

Now kids said the woods were haunted.

As we walked through the trees, pushing branches out of the way, Gus said, "I bet this place is haunted." He was always saying the obvious.

"Watch out for the bloody farmer," Tom called from up ahead. "He hides up in the trees, waiting for a victim."

"To eat?" asked Gus.

"That reminds me," I said. "I still have some lunch left. Anyone want a pickle?"

No one was hungry.

Tom and Raymond went ahead to explore, while Gus and I walked slowly.

The woods were thicker than I'd expected. Darker, too. We all froze when Raymond suddenly shouted, "You guys! Come quick!"

He was standing in a small clearing up ahead, pointing at the ground. He had a rip in his jeans and dirt all over his face.

"You have dirt all over your face," said Gus.

"I know, I know," said Raymond. "Look what I tripped over."

He pointed to a flat piece of wood in the dirt. A rusty metal handle stuck out of it. It looked like part of an old door.

"The door to the old farmer's house," whispered Tom.

"The house that was wrecked by the tornado?" asked Gus.

Raymond stood over the metal handle and kicked away some dirt with his shoe. "It's bigger," he said. We all joined in, digging and kicking at the dirt. After a minute we had uncovered the whole door.

Tom knelt down and looked hard at the handle. Underneath it was a small, round keyhole. Tom put his face close to the keyhole. He glanced up at me with a funny look.

"Garvey," he whispered. He always called me by my last name. "Put your hand over this."

I bent down and held out my hand. I felt a cool stream of air escape from the rusty keyhole.

Tom stood up. "This ain't just a door," he said. "I mean, this is a *real* door. A door with something behind it."

"It's a storm shelter," said Gus. We all stared at him. None of us had heard Gus actually come up with an idea before. "Where you hide from a tornado," he explained. "My great-grandma has one under her house."

A shelter. Where the farmer and his family hid during the storm years ago. We were all thinking the same thing. No one wanted to say it out loud. *Dead bodies.*

"Or it could be a root cellar," Gus said. "My great-grandma puts stuff in jars and keeps them in a different cellar."

"Preserves," said Raymond.

Gus nodded. "Like pickles and apples and jelly and stuff."

"Or maybe," said Tom, "it's buried treasure." He leaned down, gripped the handle, and pulled open the door. We all stepped back.

A wave of cool air rushed up out of the hole. Old wooden steps led down into darkness.

"It's dark down there," said Gus.

"Who wants to go first?" Raymond asked. No one spoke.

"Tom opened it," I said.

"Garvey's not scared," Tom said, still holding the door. "He'll go."

I nodded but didn't say anything. Now I had to go.

I walked to the top of the steps. It was impossible to see anything down there. I took a step down.

"See anything?" asked Gus.

"I'm not even down there yet," I said.

I took a few more steps. It was still too dark to see. It felt cooler.

The smell wasn't bad. It reminded me of how the grass smells after my dad mows the lawn. But there was another smell, too. It smelled like there might be animals down here.

My eyes were getting used to the darkness. I heard something squeak.

"Any treasure?" Gus called from above.

I heard a hiss from below. Then a word. "Ssssafe," I thought it said.

I was so scared, I was barely able to talk. "Wh-who's there?" I said.

"Is it . . . safe?" came the voice.

Someone lit a match, and the light from it blinded me. I saw a candle in midair. Then I saw the hand holding it. A hand that was wrinkly and covered in dirt. It had black fingernails curved like claws.

"Is the tornado gone?" asked another higher voice.

Four shadows stood in front of me. It looked like a family. A husband and wife and two children. When my eyes got used to the light, I saw that their skin hung off their bones. I had seen a mummy once on a school field trip to the museum. Their four faces looked like that. Sunken eyes. Hollow cheeks.

"That tornado's bad," said the man.

"Good thing we have this shelter," said the woman.

"Good thing we have some food down here, too," said the man. "How bad is it out there, son?" he asked.

I tried to take a step back, but the stair I was standing on broke, and I fell. "Help!" I shouted.

I heard Gus scream from above. Tom yelled a curse word and let go of the door. It dropped with a bang, and the *whoosh* of air made the candle blow out.

"Help!" I cried again. I could hear my friends shouting to each other as they ran away. I tried backing up the stairs, but they rotted and crumbled into dust. The door was too high to reach. I couldn't see a thing.

"You're safe from the storm down here," said the farmer.

"We'll stay here till it's all over," said the farmer's wife.

I heard them coming closer. It sounded like their bodies were dragging across the dirt floor.

There was another voice, quiet and mumbly. I was only able to make out a single word. "Hungry . . . hungry . . ."

The dragging sound came again from the dirt floor.

"Mumummm . . . hungry . . . ?"

The voice sounded much closer. It was the boy. The farmer's son. *Was he going to eat me?*

I heard shuffling and then the sound of metal grind against glass. A lid was being unscrewed. Then I heard the voice again. The boy's mouth was next to my ear. I could feel his warm, stinky breath.

"Are you hungry?" said the boy. "Want a pickle?"

DEAD
END

Ren was riding his bicycle late one afternoon when he saw the sign:

LOSA STREET

And under that:

DEAD END

Never saw that one, he thought.

New houses were going up all the time in his neighborhood. New houses needed new streets. And new streets were new adventures. Ren turned his bike onto the new road and pedaled faster.

He counted twenty or so empty, new houses along the way to the dead end. His dad had a fancy word for this kind of dead end — *cul-de-*

sac. In fact, Ren's family lived on a cul-de-sac. Their house was bunched up with four others around a wide, paved circle.

Ren loved to ride his bicycle around the circles — especially when he discovered a new one. When he reached the end of Losa Street, he shot around it several times without holding onto the handlebars. He felt like he was flying. Like he had wings.

Buffalo chicken wings! he thought.

His mom was making wings for dinner tonight. His favorite. Ren broke out of his circling pattern and headed back, counting the houses as he went.

He counted up to thirty. *Where is that sign?* Ren wondered. *Shouldn't I be at the end of the street by now?*

The street curved back and forth without coming to an end. Ren braked suddenly. The road had led him to another cul-de-sac. He must have missed the turn-off.

Ren headed back, and this time he pedaled harder. The late afternoon sun was setting behind the empty houses. He saw for the first time that all the houses sat behind high chain-link fences. The gates at the end of their driveways had large metal locks holding them closed. The builders probably were trying to keep curious kids away from the half-finished homes.

Ren slowed down. He couldn't believe it. He was at another cul-de-sac! It looked exactly like first one he had visited. No . . . it *was* the first! He remembered seeing those two pink houses next to each other, with the creepy troll statue in between them. How could he have missed the turn-off a second time?

Even though the air was cool, Ren was sweating. He circled the dead end and biked back the way he'd come. This time, he rode slower.

He saw that the addresses started at 40. So he counted the houses along the way as carefully as he could. Ren knew that the addresses should get lower as he got closer to the entrance to the street.

Where is the sign that says Losa Street? he wondered.

Finally, Ren saw it. The back of the sign. He rode closer. *Wait a second . . .* Ren thought. It was the other sign. *DEAD END.* And that's exactly what he found beyond it. The other cul-de-sac.

It didn't make sense. A street with two dead ends?

He had been counting the houses. Reading the shiny new address numbers nailed beside each door. The numbers got lower . . . 17 . . . 13 . . . 11 . . . 9 . . . 5 . . . then they stopped. And there was the dead end.

But wait! Ren pedaled down the street the other way again, counting the numbers as they got higher. As he pedaled, he saw that the highest address was 37. But Ren was sure that last time he'd pedaled here, the houses had started at 40.

Ren began to worry. He rode back again, counting the numbers out loud.

This time, 5 and 9 were gone.

What's going on? Houses are vanishing . . . Ren thought.

The street was getting shorter. The sun was moving lower in the sky behind the row of empty buildings.

"Hey!" Ren yelled. His voice echoed along the street.

He thought he heard dogs barking. Ren followed the sound, but it only led him back to the first cul-de-sac. And he didn't come across any dogs there.

Maybe I'm dreaming, Ren thought. *Maybe I fell off my bike and hit my head. That's it! I must be imagining things. If I get off my bike, walk, and take some deep breaths, I'll feel better.*

He hopped off his bike and began to walk back and forth slowly on the dark street, holding onto the handlebars of his bike. *In real life,* Ren thought, *every street has a beginning and end. It has to. Otherwise, how would people get home?*

When Ren felt a little better, he looked up ahead again. But what he saw was the thing he most feared.

The street was so short that he could see both cul-de-sacs. They were facing each other. The street was getting narrower, too. The fences on both sides were closer.

Ren wiped the sweat off his forehead and blinked. When he opened his eyes, there was no longer a street . . . only one dead end. A high chain-link fence surrounded him. He felt like a bird trapped in a cage.

Ren dropped his bike onto the asphalt. He ran up to one of the locked gates and shook it. "Hey!" he yelled at the house on the other side. "Hey, someone! Is there someone there?"

The windows of the house stared back at him like black, empty eyes.

"Hello? Anyone?" he called.

Ren thought about climbing the fence. But he looked up and saw there was barbed wire at the top. Plus, he felt so tired.

Ren turned and walked back to his bike. His bike? It was gone.

He stood alone inside the circle, inside the fence.

Ren looked up. The sunlight was fading. His strength was fading, too. The last ray of sunlight hit a sign hanging on the fence. It was the sign he had seen when he first turned onto Losa Street. *DEAD END*. He was sure it was the same sign.

Except now, one of the words was gone.

THE DOLL THAT WAVED GOODBYE

Livia wore a doll's hand around her neck.

The doll had first belonged to Livia's grandmother. She had passed it down to Livia's mother, who had then given it to Livia. Over the years, the doll's green silk dress had grown worn and tattered. It had lost an arm when Livia's mother and aunt fought over the doll as children. Livia's cat had scratched the head and ripped off its real human hair that was tied in tiny braids. Piece by piece, the little doll had fallen apart. Finally, only the left hand remained, and Livia now wore it as a necklace.

Livia had explained this to the other girls on her first night at summer camp. The girls in her cabin were getting ready for bed when one of them, Emily, saw something moving at Livia's throat. It was the hand, swinging on its chain.

The girls all looked closer at the little hand.

"It's porcelain," Livia said.

"That's what my grandma's teacups are made of," said another girl, Amber.

Livia nodded. "It's very delicate."

All the girls could see that the little hand had tiny cracks running through it. The fingernails had faded from red to pink. A thin bracelet of gold wire wrapped around the doll's wrist. Another wire with a little hoop on the end stuck out of the wrist like a skinny bone. A chain ran through the hoop and hooked around Livia's neck.

Her cabin mates "oohed" and "ahhed" over the doll hand. A few of them asked to touch the white fingers, but Livia shook her head. "I'm sorry," she said. "But it's quite delicate. It's so old. And I'm so afraid it might break."

All of the girls understood. All except for Brooke.

Why can't I touch the doll hand? Brooke wondered as she sat in bed that night. *Just touching it once won't hurt.*

All night, while the others slept soundly in their bunks, Brooke stared at the bunk above hers. She was angry with Livia. Brooke hated snobby people, and she thought Livia was one of the worst. *So scared of letting anyone touch her stupid, precious doll,* thought Brooke. *Not even a doll. Only a stupid hand.*

But the more Brooke thought about it, the more she wanted to try on Livia's necklace. *Anyway, why shouldn't she touch it? Why not wear it?* It would only be for a minute. Half a minute. What was wrong with that?

But Brooke knew Livia would never give her permission, so she waited. All week she waited to find the necklace lying on the little table next to Livia's bunk. Or on her pillow. As the days rolled by at camp, however, Brooke learned that Livia never took off the doll hand. She wore it in the morning to the Sing-Fest. She wore it during crafting class. She wore it on the bird-watching hike. When the rest of the campers went swimming in the lake, Livia sat on the shore and read. She said the water could ruin the porcelain.

Every night as Livia got ready for bed, Brooke saw her pat the doll hand to make sure it was still there before she slipped into her bed to sleep.

Brooke grew angrier and angrier. *Who does Livia think she is, anyway? People are supposed to share. They're supposed to take turns.*

It just wasn't fair, Brooke thought, that she couldn't hold the doll necklace in her hands. Or feel it around her neck.

Late one night, when everyone in the cabin was asleep, Brooke threw back the cover of her sleeping bag and crept out of her bunk. It only took a few steps to reach the side of Livia's bunk. Brooke stood there, looking down at the sleeping snobby girl. It was hard to see in the darkness of the cabin. She bent closer toward Livia's neck.

Brooke gasped. She covered her mouth with her hands, afraid the sound might wake the sleeping girl.

The chain hung around Livia's neck as it always did, but the doll hand was gone.

Goose bumps ran up and down the back of Brooke's neck. She hurried back to her bunk and squirmed into her sleeping bag. She shivered, even under the thick cover. Why did the sight of the bare necklace frighten her? Perhaps the hand had slipped off while Livia slept, and it was hidden under her hair or her T-shirt.

Brooke closed her eyes and tried to calm down.

That was close, she thought. If her gasp had woken up Livia, what would she have said? What excuse would she have made up?

Just then, Brooke heard a tiny sound on the side of her bed. A soft, metallic sound. *Zzzzz.* The sound grew slightly louder, closer. *Zzzzz.* It reminded Brooke of a zipper.

Someone — or something — was zipping up her sleeping bag.

Brooke forced herself to open her eyes. But no one was standing beside her bed. All the girls were sleeping in their bunks.

The zipping stopped, but another sound took its place. Scratching. She felt something small crawling down her sleeping bag toward the foot of the bunk. Brooke thought of mice and almost screamed, but then the crawling stopped.

She took a deep breath. The sound returned, coming from the post of the bunk. It climbed up the post to the bunk above her. It stopped for a moment, but then it moved again.

Brooke saw a tiny shadow moving on the underside of the bunk above her. A mouse? A moth?

The shadow grew wider, as if a tiny hand were spreading its fingers.

Suddenly, a white hand fell from above and landed on Brooke's mouth. Its cold fingers grew and grew. Soon it was as large as a human hand. The hand was covered in cracks with pale pink fingernails.

Worst of all, the hand was strong enough to keep anyone from hearing Brooke cry out.

* * *

"Brooke's gone!"

Livia and the other girls woke up the following morning to Emily's cry. They were surprised to see Brooke's belongings all packed up. Her sleeping bag was rolled up neatly and resting on the floor. A few minutes later, the camp counselor came in, followed by Brooke who picked up her suitcase and bag and left without saying a word.

On her way out the door, the camp counselor turned to the speechless campers and whispered, "I think Brooke misses home. She had a bad night." Then she quietly closed the door behind her.

"She didn't even say goodbye," said Amber.

"What do you think happened?" asked Emily.

Livia giggled softly. Too softly for the others to hear. She wasn't laughing because Brooke was leaving. She was laughing as if she was being tickled. As if something small and delicate was wiggling near her throat. As if something small was waving goodbye.

HALLOWEEN
HEAD

Oliver stood on the dark lawn while laughter and movement and flashing cell phones whirled around him. Throngs of kids were walking up and down the sidewalks, crossing the streets, laughing and talking cheerfully. They lifted their masks to talk to each other. They bent their heads to check out the goodies in each other's trick-or-treat bags. A few of the more eager kids sucked on lollipops or chewed on chocolate bars.

Oliver stood quietly, without moving a muscle. He was staring at something, or rather someone, at the end of the street.

A kid in a fat bumblebee costume ran up to him. "Ollie! Look at the score from the

Hansons' house! They give you three different candy bars!"

Normally this kind of news would make Oliver's eyes pop and his saliva glands go into overdrive. But Oliver didn't move. He held up a finger to silence his friend. "Joseph," he said quietly. "Take a look down the street."

Joseph looked. Then he shrugged. "So? It's just some kid."

"But who is he?" said Oliver.

"Some big teenager who wants candy," said Joseph. "That must be why he's only wearing a mask. He's too cool."

Weird mask, thought Oliver. The tall teenager, wearing a T-shirt, a jacket, and jeans, was also wearing a paper grocery bag over his head with two small slits for eyeholes.

"But I haven't seen him go up to any house," said Oliver. "And he's not carrying a bag for candy."

Joseph clutched his own bag more tightly to his bumblebee body. "Do you think he steals candy from other people? He's not getting mine! No way!" Then he sprinted off the lawn and down the sidewalk, away from the masked teenager.

He's not getting mine either, thought Oliver. *Candy is my life.* Halloween was the only time of year when Oliver could get mountains of candy absolutely free. He wasn't going to let this night go to waste.

The shadowy figure wearing the bag shifted back and forth on his feet. He seemed impatient, wanting to move.

Oliver had three or four more blocks to hit before he headed home. Then he'd be in his own bedroom and wouldn't have to think about the weird kid wearing the bag. But after the next house, Oliver noticed the teenager standing under the streetlight across the street. Then after the second house, he saw him standing in the yard next door. And after the third house, when Oliver's bag was growing almost too heavy with its sugary loot, the teen stood on the sidewalk just in front of the house next-door.

The masked figure was waiting.

Oliver thought of copying his bumblebee pal, Joseph, and running toward home, dashing through his neighbors' front yards.

But instead, he grew angry. He was afraid of this stranger following him, and the fear made him mad. *Who is this guy anyway?*

Oliver wondered. *Why is he following me? There's no way I'm giving up my candy.*

A full moon hung in the dark October sky, white as a marshmallow. It was very late, and most trick-or-treaters had gone home. Oliver could hear voices a few blocks away. The faint sound of closing doors. Dying laughter and screams.

There was no one else on the block but him and the masked teen. If the older kid tried to grab Oliver's bag or knock him down and run, there was nobody around to witness it or run after the thief. He could always scream, but Oliver felt that screaming was for wimps.

Oliver hoisted up his bag, walked down the sidewalk, and headed toward his shadowy stalker.

He stopped a few feet away from the teen. His legs felt like they were made of licorice, but he stood up tall. "What's the big deal?" Oliver asked angrily. "Why do you keep following me?"

The grocery bag tilted down toward Oliver. But the teen did not answer.

"Who are you?" asked Oliver. The tiny slits stared at him, but the teen still didn't make a sound. "Can't you talk?"

The masked figure slowly swayed back and forth, shifting his weight from one foot to the other. He didn't make any move toward Oliver. He simply stared.

"Just leave me alone," said Oliver. He held onto his bag with both hands and started walking past the teen. The teen did not back out of the way in time. Oliver brushed against his jacket. He braced himself, expecting a hand to dart out and shove him to the sidewalk, but nothing happened.

Oliver turned around quickly. Anger boiled up inside of him. And then, without thinking or planning, Oliver reached up and snatched at the paper bag. "Who are you?!"

Oliver heard a high-pitched scream. Then he realized it was coming from his own wide-open mouth. With the paper bag in his hand, he stared at the teen and saw there was no head on his shoulders. Not even a neck.

The figure started to wave his arms around blindly, searching for his bag with the slits for eyeholes. He stumbled off the sidewalk and onto the street.

Suddenly, there was another high-pitched sound. Squealing brakes. The headless figure fell in front of a car and smashed onto the road. Oliver watched, frozen with fear. He watched as the teen's body seemed to crumple like paper. His skin rippled open, like a popped balloon, spilling a thousand pieces of candy onto the asphalt, glittering in the car's headlights. Red and pink and white, like blood and skin and bones.

The man driving the car and the woman in the passenger's seat jumped out. "What happened?" he yelled.

"You hit someone! You hit someone!" the woman shrieked.

The man shook his head, staring at the mass of candy gleaming in the headlights.

"Hey, kid!" he shouted to Oliver. "You saw what happened, right?"

Oliver got out of there fast. He ran through the dark spaces under the trees and stumbled across his neighbors' yards. His eyes were glazed. His hand was glued to his bag.

After a few blocks, his feet hit a sidewalk. He blinked and saw that he was close to his house. On this block, a few kids were still running up to houses, pressing doorbells and yelling for treats.

A kid in a werewolf costume started to walk past Oliver, but Oliver stopped him. "Hey," he said. "Do you like candy?"

"Who doesn't?" said the werewolf.

Oliver handed him his candy bag. "Take it," he said. "I don't eat the stuff anymore."

Then Oliver turned and walked toward his house, without realizing he was still tightly clutching the other bag, the one with slits for eyeholes. And the slits were staring at his head.

NIGHT CRAWLERS

Two boys on bikes appeared from a line of trees by a lonely lake. They braked a few feet from the water's edge.

"I don't hear anything," whispered Sean, the first boy.

"No one lives around here," said the other boy, Jeremy. "Nice and quiet."

The lake was an almost perfect circle, surrounded by a wide shore and a thick band of trees. The still water reflected the sky above, making the lake look like a vast blue hole. A hole as endless as space.

Sean watched a few white clouds drift across the water's surface.

"Does your brother still fish here?" Sean asked.

Jeremy shook his head. "He never fished here. He just heard about it from some guy at school. I don't think many people come here. No real roads lead here — just the trail."

The boys got off their bikes and slid their heavy backpacks onto the ground. They set up the tent, rolled out their sleeping bags, and organized their gear. They were unpacking their fishing rods when Sean noticed a dark, low shape on the lake. He thought it was moving. The boys continued to unpack their supplies but kept an eye on the shape. It grew larger as it neared the shore. Both boys jumped up and ran toward the water.

It was a small, gray rowboat. Large enough for two passengers, but no one was inside.

"The oars are still inside," said Jeremy.

"How did it get here?" said Sean. "There's no wind."

"It drifted," said Jeremy. He waded out a few feet and grabbed a rope at the front of the boat. He and Sean and dragged it onto the shore.

Jeremy frowned. "You think someone fell out and drowned?" he asked.

"We didn't hear anything," said Sean.

Jeremy cupped his hands to his mouth and shouted. His echo rang loudly through the forest, across the lake and back again. There was no reply. "If someone was yelling before we got here, we would have heard it out on the trail," said Jeremy.

"Dead man's boat," Sean muttered to himself.

Jeremy swatted at a mosquito. "Don't get weird," he said. "It's old. It's probably been out here a long time. We can't do anything now, anyway. We're all set up."

Sean slowly nodded and rubbed his arms. The air was getting cooler, and the sun was lower in the sky. *We may as well stay and have some fun,* he thought.

It was too late to start fishing, so the boys built a small fire and cooked hot dogs and pizza rolls for dinner. Shadows deepened around their tent as they drank sodas and ate candy bars. When the sun had almost set and the sky was turning the color of cheddar cheese, Jeremy grabbed a flashlight. "Now's the fun part," he said.

"Night crawlers!" they both yelled.

Sean grabbed his own flashlight and an empty bucket. Carrying shovels and swinging their beams from side to side, they carefully made their way into the woods. The boys considered night crawlers, or earthworms, the best bait around. Digging up the worms themselves, instead of paying for them at a bait shop, always made them feel like true outdoorsmen. Tonight they'd hunt for night crawlers and use them to fish in the lake.

Jeremy stopped and stamped on the moist earth. He set his foot on the shovel and pushed down with all his weight. Sean did the same.

"The worms are supposed to be nice and fat here," said Jeremy, puffing a little as he dug. "They don't call this place Night Crawler Lake for nothing."

"You said this lake didn't have a name," said Sean.

Jeremy shrugged, but kept turning over the rich, black soil. "That's just a nickname."

With their flashlights, the boys scanned the dirt. Dozens of pinkish worms, thick as fingers, squirmed and wriggled.

"What did I tell ya?" said Jeremy. He scooped up handfuls of worms and dropped them in the bucket. He nodded. "Nice," he said.

It wasn't long before the bucket was overflowing with thick, juicy night crawlers.

"You were right about this place," said Sean.

"C'mon, let's get some more," said Jeremy, heading farther into the woods.

"We've got plenty," said Sean.

Jeremy ignored him. "I want a few more," he said, and he kept walking.

Sean followed, but he wasn't happy about it. Soon, he heard Jeremy exclaim, "These are the best! Look, Sean. Look how big they are."

Sean had to admit the new worms lying at his friend's feet were huge — pink, wet sausages.

Jeremy bent over to pick them up. He quickly dropped them with a shout. He pointed with his shaking flashlight. "Not . . . not worms . . ."

It was a man's hand. Chopped off neatly at the wrist.

"My — my shovel must have cut it off," Jeremy said.

Sean felt sick to his stomach. "But what's it doing out —"

The fingers moved. Both boys jumped back. In the fresh hole that Jeremy had dug, the dirt was stirring. A second hand, this one attached to a muddy arm, reached up from the ground.

The boys dropped their shovels and flashlights and darted behind a tree trunk. The arm was followed by a shoulder and then a man's head. Then his entire torso. Silently, the man pulled himself free from the ground. He raised himself to all fours and crawled slowly across the ground, his head moving from side to side as if he was searching for something. Heavy, wet earth dripped from his body.

The forest filled with rustling sounds. As their eyes adjusted to the dark, Sean and Jeremy could faintly see another shape moving along the ground about twenty feet away. A second man crawling slowly along the forest floor.

Jeremy gripped his shoulder. "Look over there," he said.

Another figure was struggling out of the ground behind the first two. Leaves and twigs rustled as the crawlers moved over them. Sean counted seven more figures digging their way out of the damp soil. He thought one or two might be women, because of their long hair hanging down, hair that was streaked with mud and leaves.

Something rustled at their feet. The boys turned and saw two hands reaching up through the dirt. Five more shadows gathered a few yards away. All the shadows were crawling toward them.

The boys didn't care if they made any noise as they fled back toward the lake. They saw more and more people crawling among the trees, moving silently toward them.

"I told you we had enough worms!" yelled Sean. "You should have stopped."

Jeremy cupped his hands to his mouth and shouted for help. His echo died in the empty air.

Crash!

Several of the crawlers had plowed through the boys' tent, knocking over their bikes and their supplies. The crawlers moved as if in a trance, not caring what stood in their way. There were dozens of them, caked in mud. Rotting clothes hung in tatters from their stiff bodies. The boys kept backing up, until they felt the lake water at their ankles.

"The boat," said Jeremy.

They jumped into the rowboat, grabbed the oars, and began rowing away from the shore.

"We should be safe out here, right?" Jeremy asked, breathing hard.

Twenty or more crawlers had stopped at the lake's edge, sniffing at the water. Then they pushed ahead. The creatures splashed into the lake and soon disappeared underwater. Once the first line of crawlers slid under, another came close behind. It seemed the forest would never run out of them. Like a swarm of oversized army ants, the creatures crawled into the lake.

Jeremy and Sean rowed farther away. In his panic, Jeremy lost hold of his oar and dropped it in the water. Instead of floating, as it should have done, the oar quickly sank out of sight. Sean tried to row even harder with the remaining oar, but he only succeeded in making them turn in circles.

"Wait," said Jeremy. "They're gone."

The shore was empty. Nothing moved under the trees. The lake was silent and peaceful.

"Let's go back," said Jeremy. "We'll get our bikes and go."

Goose bumps ran up and down Sean's bare arms. "There's something wrong," he said. He gazed over the edge of the rowboat. The rippling water was black as oil. The boat gently bobbed up and down like an Adam's apple in a swallowing throat.

"No, no," said Sean. "This is all wrong."

"What are you talking about?" said Jeremy.

"There are no bubbles," said Sean.

"So?"

"No one's breathing," said Sean. "They don't need air!"

Before Jeremy could respond, Sean's oar was ripped from his grasp. The boat rocked as if hundreds of hands were pushing and shoving and guiding the boat farther and farther from shore. The boys didn't shout for help. They knew no one would hear them. After all, they hadn't heard anyone yelling when they'd arrived at the lake.

By the time the moon rose above the trees, the boat was empty. The lake was quiet. But under the oily waves, shadows squirmed and wriggled, like a thousand hungry night crawlers.

CHALK

A huge, gross monster with bloody fangs and seven horns took up the entire driveway.

Jordan was returning from a bike ride with his friends. When he turned into the driveway, he saw the monster and braked. His younger sister, Nyla, was on her hands and knees, resting on the creature's belly. The belly, like every other part of the creature, was bone white. Nyla was finishing the last row of scales when she heard Jordan behind her.

"What is all this?" Jordan asked.

Nyla looked up. A skinny white object rested in her hand.

"It's my pet dragon," she said.

"Are you nuts? Dad said no drawing on the driveway," Jordan said.

Nyla shrugged and returned to drawing. "Daddy will think my dragon is beautiful," she said.

"Daddy will ground you and send you to your room," said Jordan. Their father was an architect and worked from home. When people visited him during the day, he wanted to impress them with their beautiful house that he had designed. A messy driveway was a bad first impression.

Nyla kept drawing.

Jordan had to admit that the dragon looked awesome. He didn't know Nyla was such a good artist. It must have taken her hours to draw that dragon. It was full of details like the blood dripping from its teeth, the sharp lines of its three white eyes, and a curling tail with hundreds of scales. The whole drawing must have been fifteen feet long.

"How long have you been out here?" Jordan asked.

"A few minutes," Nyla said.

"You're lying," Jordan said.

"Am not!" cried Nyla.

"Nobody could draw all this in a few minutes," Jordan pointed out.

"But I did!" said Nyla, frowning at him. "The poor lady said it was special chalk."

"What lady?" asked Jordan.

Nyla held up a small wooden box. "She gave me this."

Jordan dropped his bike on the grass and walked over to grab the box.

"She said I could draw pretty things with the chalk," Nyla said.

The red wooden box felt light in Jordan's hands. He saw that there were tiny drawings carved into the wood. There were sharp brass thingies at the corners that poked his hands.

"The poor lady walked away, and then you came," said Nyla.

Jordan opened the box.

"The poor lady said it was a present," said Nyla.

In the bottom of the box lay four long pieces of chalk. They looked like the one Nyla was using. Jordan picked one up for a closer look. Startled, he dropped the box and the piece of chalk on the grass. But they weren't pieces of chalk. They were fingers. Skeleton fingers.

Nyla smiled at her dragon.

"The poor lady was so nice," said Nyla.

Jordan could hardly breathe. "Why do you keep calling her 'the poor lady'?"

"I feel sorry for her," said Nyla as she kept drawing. "She only had one hand."

SIDEWALKS FROM OUTER SPACE

What a movie! I mean, what a *movie!*

We burst out of the theater — my friend Carlos and I, and my big brother, Caleb, and his buddy Ethan. We couldn't stop talking about it.

"Awesome, dude!" Carlos said.

"Totally awesome," I said.

Stealth Invasion IV: Alien Destruction. Best. Movie. Ever. The absolute best in the series.

"I want to see it again," said Caleb.

"We are so seeing it again," said Carlos.

"I can't," said Ethan. "Gotta get home. It's late."

It was late. After midnight. The moon and stars were shining. My mom and Carlos's parents had let us stay out late because we were with Caleb and Ethan, who were sixteen.

We walked down the sidewalk, past a corner where people were getting on a city bus. Its doors hissed shut as it pulled away from the curb. The greenish lights inside the bus and the tinted windows made the passengers inside look like aliens. Visitors to our planet were taking off in their silver ship. *Swoosh!*

"The alien destructor suits were cool!" I said.

"Their blue starships were even cooler," said Carlos.

Caleb snorted. "Which is why the whole thing would never work," he said. "Not in real life. Not in a million years."

"Yeah," said Ethan.

I stopped walking. "What do you mean?" I said.

"Alien invasion," said Caleb. "If their ships were coming at us like that, in the open, we would have seen them from miles away."

"The armies of Earth would have banded together," said Ethan. "By the time they reached the planet, we'd be ready for them."

"We sure wouldn't be surprised, like the army dudes in the movie," said Caleb. "The movie's called *Stealth Invasion*. Where was the stealth part?"

"Good one, dude," agreed Ethan.

We started walking again. We were ten blocks from our house. Carlos was sleeping over with us, but Ethan lived a little farther away. The four of us were the only ones on the sidewalk. I could feel warmth rising from the cement, even though the night was cool. Cool and dark. And each block got darker than the last. Why weren't the streetlights working?

Ethan was chuckling to himself. I guess he was still thinking about Caleb's remark that the aliens weren't stealthy. Caleb sort of had a point.

"If you're so smart, how would you do it?" asked Carlos.

"Yeah, how would you do it?" I said.

Caleb usually waves his arms around when he talks big. This time he didn't. He stopped in the middle of the block, where the shadows were thickest. He leaned in close to us, like he didn't want anyone else to hear. "Like the movie says, boys — stealth," Caleb said. "Hidden. Secret. Camouflaged."

"I know what stealth means," I said.

"If I were an alien, I'd already be here," said Caleb. "I would have been here for years by now. Dozens of years. Hiding. Just waiting for the right time. Then I'd attack and catch everyone by surprise. That's how an invasion works."

"Good one, dude," said Ethan.

"Where would you hide?" Carlos asked quietly.

Caleb looked around. He stared down at his shoes. He snorted again. "We don't know what aliens really look like, right?" he said. "So why couldn't they be disguised as something normal you see everyday?"

"Something normal?" said Ethan seriously.

Caleb nodded. "Like . . . a sidewalk."

Carlos laughed. Ethan didn't smile.

A sidewalk, I thought. *Why not?*

"One night," said Caleb. "When we were all asleep, the aliens came. The aliens were long like giant snakes. Their scales were hard like cement. They took the place of sidewalks all over town. All across the country. And all those years while we were walking on them, they were listening and watching. Learning all about us humans. And we might never ever know."

How long would the aliens wait to attack? I wondered.

"Let's go home," said Carlos.

But I had to know more. "When would you attack?" I asked.

"Tonight," said Ethan. "No one would be expecting that. Would they?"

Caleb looked at him in surprise.

"You guys are creeping me out," said Carlos.

I looked at the sidewalk. I tried feeling it through my shoes. Was it warmer than normal? Sidewalks stayed warm after it got dark, because they held all that heat from the sun. But was that really the reason, or were they actually alive? I stared at the sidewalk in the dark. I tried to tell if it was moving. If it was breathing.

Caleb was biting his upper lip. I knew that look. He was trying hard not to laugh. I ignored him and looked up at the night sky. There were a lot of shooting stars.

"You guys . . ." said Carlos.

The sidewalk shook, like an earthquake or something really big was happening.

Something really big, but really far away, and just now reaching us.

"We're just feeling a truck go by," said Caleb.

"There aren't any trucks on the street," Ethan pointed out. There weren't any cars either. It was dark, and we were the only ones around.

"Can this be happening?" I said.

I looked at the street again. Was Caleb right? No one would suspect a sidewalk. You saw them every day. Wait! I glanced at the corner of the block.

The fire hydrant was glowing. Slowly it stretched up into the air, growing like a weird metal tree.

"That's how they did it!" said Caleb. "That's their disguise!"

Ethan stood right behind me, chuckling. "Don't be stupid," he said. "Hydrants aren't alive."

The hydrant grew taller and thicker until it was the size of a car.

Suddenly, Ethan's voice changed. "They're things," he said. "Tools."

I turned around and saw a stranger wearing Ethan's clothes. His body was heavy. His arms ended in claws. His face was green and rubbery. His eyes were just slits, like a cat's.

"What do you see every day?" he said, in a thick, rubbery voice. "Your friends," he went on. "Your neighbors. But do you really know who they are? What they are?"

The stranger came closer, and the three of us, Caleb, Carlos, and I, backed up farther and farther.

Something metal clanged. Bars fell in front of us like a jail cell. We were locked inside the hydrant. It had become a sturdy steel cage.

That's when we heard the sirens go off.

And when we knew the aliens were here.

SNOW MONSTER

The sun was low in the sky. The clouds were so orange, they looked like they were on fire. There was a light breeze. The snow had stopped falling. It was perfect hunting weather.

Deer come out right before the sun sets. And there are a lot of deer where we live, just outside a small town in northern Wisconsin. North of our home there's a line of evergreens, which is the border of a large forest. Lots of deer trails lead into the trees. We were following one that morning.

I love being out in the woods with my father. When I was really young, he taught me how to recognize an animal's footprints.

In the woods that morning I could see the tracks of rabbits, fox, field mice, and, of course, deer.

It was cold enough to see our breath, but not too cold. Carefully and quietly we headed deep into the woods. We came to a small clearing. My father stopped suddenly.

He was looking down at the snow. "We'd better go back, son," he said.

"What is it?" I asked.

He shook his head and turned away, but I had to see. I ran over and looked at the snow. There were footprints I had never seen before. They were huge — at least four times bigger than my father's.

I looked at him. *The Geeshee Moogomon?* I wondered.

I had heard the stories. The Geeshee was a big, bloodthirsty beast that could change its shape and color. You never saw it until it was too late. It was a story adults told us to keep us from going into the deep woods. To keep us out of trouble. I'd never believed it was real.

My father was firm. "We're going home," he said. "Now."

Suddenly, I saw what else my father had seen. The dead body. A deer had fallen onto the snow.

Blood spread out from it, red staining the white ground.

A scream pierced the air. A nearby tree seemed to explode. Bark flew off and hit my head.

"Hurry!" cried my father.

We both turned and took off across the snow, our tails flying behind us. I never looked back.

After several minutes, my father stopped. He lifted his head and howled. We had to warn our cousins and neighbors of the danger.

We took the long way home. "So the Geeshee won't be able to find us," my father said.

When we were finally inside our den, I raced to my mother. I snuggled as close as I could, hearing her heart beat beneath her beautiful fur.

For now, I was safe from the monster.

SECTION 3

OUT OF YOUR MIND

BLINK!

The eye doctor puts drops in my eyes.

"This won't hurt," he says. And he's right. It doesn't hurt at all. There's a funny stinging on my eyeballs, but that's all.

"This is a new medicine," he says. "It should clear up that infection really quickly."

He's talking about the weird eye infection I got at school. Lots of kids were getting it — even a few teachers. It makes green crud come out of your eyes, and everything looks fuzzy. So my mom took me to see our eye doctor, Dr. Glass, this morning. I know. Glass. Funny, right?

"Don't rub your eyes for at least an hour," says the doctor.

My mom is leading me out of the office when Dr. G. stops us. "Oh, one other thing, Kevin," he says to me. "There's a little side effect."

"Side effect?" I repeat.

"You might feel a little dizzy," Dr. Glass says as he carefully reads the label on the bottle of medicine he dropped into my eyes just a minute ago.

Didn't he check it out before? I wonder. And suddenly I'm not feeling great about my visit.

"It seems you'll have double vision," he says. "It should wear off in a few hours. Nothing to worry about."

"Double vision?" I ask. I'm about to say, *What does that mean?* But suddenly I'm staring at two doctors, each holding a bottle in their right hand. *Okay,* I think. *I know what it means.*

My mom leads me out of the doctor's office, down the hall, and into the elevator. I hate elevators, but Dr. Glass's office is on the twenty-third floor of the medical building downtown. There's no way I'd be able to climb down twenty-three flights of stairs.

My eyes feel hot. I start to rub them, but then my mom says, "Remember what the doctor said. Don't rub your eyes."

"They itch," I reply.

"Try not to think about it," she says.

"I'm *not* thinking about it," I say. "And they still itch."

"Hush!" she says, glancing around the elevator car. She's looking at the two other passengers, embarrassed.

I close my eyes, but they start to sting. When I open them again, the elevator has two more passengers.

Weird. I don't remember the elevator stopping. I didn't hear the little ding it makes when it stops at a floor. I didn't hear the footsteps of people getting on.

My eyes are hot, so I blink again. Now I see eight people in the elevator. *Oh yeah, double vision,* I remind myself. *My eyes are playing tricks.*

But the people in the elevator are acting odd. I hear a woman gasp. A man says, "Let me off! Now!"

Blink.

Now the elevator is almost full. And what's even weirder, there are lots of people wearing the same clothes. Like they're clones or something. At first I thought it was just my eyes acting funny because of the drops. But people are starting to cram in tighter and tighter, so maybe there really are more people on the elevator.

Blink.

Without warning, I'm shoved up against the wall.

"Where are all these people coming from?" cries my mother.

And I realize I'm not only *seeing* doubles. There *are* doubles. Doubles of doubles. The number of passengers is doubling, and then doubling again. Each time I blink, more people pop into view. It isn't my eyes. It's really happening.

This is the most amazing thing that has ever happened to me. I can't help myself. I have to look again.

Blink.

Not a good idea.

I get pushed into a corner of the elevator. The air is stuffy, and someone just farted. Great.

"Push the stop button!" someone yells.

"Move your elbow!" says another.

"I can't reach the buttons," says a third. "It's too crowded."

How many people are there? How many bodies can the elevator hold? At least it feels like the elevator is still going down.

Thud.

The elevator stops. We're stuck between floors!

"Kevin!" I hear my mom's voice.

"I'm back here," I reply. I don't dare to look at her. I keep my eyes squeezed shut.

Four men near the front of the elevator all say at the same time, "We're on the main floor. This is the lobby. But the doors won't open."

Four women say, "Push the Open button."

Four more women say, "Can whoever is farting please stop?"

Eight men say, "It wasn't me!"

It's getting harder to breathe. We're running out of air. I can feel bodies squirming around me. I can hear people crying, shouting, moaning, giggling. (Some people are ticklish, I guess.)

"Kevin!" My mom's voice is getting weaker.

"I'm going to faint," a man next to me says.

Somewhere a woman whispers, "What we need is more force to open those doors."

Force! I think. More and more power pushing against the doors. This gives me an idea. It might be foolish, but I figure we can't stay in the elevator much longer. We need to get out one way or another.

I open my eyes.

I look at as many people as I can. Then I blink. And I keep on blinking.

More and more bodies fill the elevator. Bodies on top of bodies. Screaming bodies. Squirming bodies. The ceiling light is covered up, then it gets smashed in the squeeze. My knees are giving out from all the extra people weighing me down. The air is being sucked up faster and faster by the extra pairs of lungs.

A long, drawn-out groan shakes the elevator. And then — *bang!* — the crush of people burst the elevator doors apart. It worked! We spill out into the lobby like candy from a gumball machine.

My mom finds me after a few minutes. She hugs me and then grabs my arm and walks me outside.

"My eyes hurt!" I say. "I can't open them."

"That's fine, sweetie," she says.

She gets us onto a bus and back home safely, guiding me the whole way.

Alone in my room, I feel my way over to the bed. I figure I'll lie down, pull the covers over my head, and rest. Dr. Glass said the double vision would last a few hours. If I go to sleep now, when I wake up in the morning everything should be back to normal.

My feet hit something as I walk across the floor, and I stumble. My eyes fly open. Oh no!

I was looking at my bed when I fell. It didn't double. It looks a little fuzzy around the edges, but otherwise it has stayed the same the same.

That was lucky, I think. I sit on the edge of the bed and stare across the room at my dresser. The dresser with the mirror.

Blink.

Big mistake.

Too bad there aren't two beds in my room. I could use them now.

I mean, *we* could.

A
PERFECT
FIT

Fitting in. That's the hardest part about going to a new school, Lola thought.

New hallways, new teachers, new locker — all of it was hard at first. But fitting in and finding new friends was the worst.

And the worst part of fitting in, Lola thought, *is figuring out where to sit for lunch.* It was the biggest decision of her first day. Lola couldn't afford to make a mistake.

Standing near the wall of the cafeteria, Lola held her lunch tray and looked around. She was too new to have made any friends. No one expected her to sit with them. Lola was afraid to sit just anywhere. What if she sat at the wrong table? With the wrong kids, kids who also didn't fit in? For the rest of her middle school life, she would be known as a loser.

"Hey! Hey you!" Lola saw a girl in a bright-yellow sweater waving at her. She slowly walked over to the girl's table.

"You mean *me?*" asked Lola.

"Sit down," said the girl in the yellow sweater. "I'm Jordan." Then she introduced the other four girls at the table: Eva, Anna, Lillian, and Kate.

"And what is your name?" asked Jordan.

"Lola," she said, shyly.

"Lola? That's different," said Anna.

The girl named Lillian giggled.

"It's Spanish," said Eva. "Or Mexican."

"Oh. Are you, like, Mexican?" asked Kate.

Eva rolled her eyes.

"No," said Lola. "My mom just liked the name."

Jordan nodded. "It's very Hollywood," she said.

Lunchtime passed quickly. The girls talked about classes and teachers and what they had done over summer vacation. The cafeteria bell rang. Lola looked up at the caged clock. Lunch period was over? She was having so much fun that she hadn't noticed the time.

"Time to go, girls," said a teacher as she walked by.

When they got up from the table, Lola noticed something for the first time. Something odd. Each girl wore the same backpack. The backpacks were purple with white trim. Some of the girls had decorated theirs with stickers and key chains and buttons, but it was the same backpack.

As she gathered her own bag, Lola realized that all the girls had worn them while they ate. None of them had taken their backpacks off.

Maybe they're a club, thought Lola. *And that's, like, their uniform or something.*

"See ya," said Lola, with a little wave.

"Bye!" they all replied brightly. The five girls turned and walked away from the table. Five purple backpacks disappeared into the crowd of students.

For the next week, Lola always sat at the same table. She sometimes saw her lunch pals in the halls. She had classes with a few of them. Jordan (the girl who had waved at her), Anna, Eva, Lillian, and Kate. No matter where she saw them, they always wore their backpacks. Even while sitting in class.

What about PE class? Lola wondered. *They'd have to put them in their lockers then, right?*

One day, Lola heard two other girls in the hall talking about her friends.

"Those backpack girls are so fake," said one.

"They act all sweet," agreed the other one. "But then they say things behind your back."

Lola didn't think her new friends were fake. They had gone out of their way to be nice to her, to make her feel welcome. And they didn't gossip any more than everyone else did. Those girls in the hall were just jealous.

During Friday's lunch, when all the girls were seated, Anna leaned into the table and whispered, "Tomorrow night — sleepover!"

"Cool!"

"Yeah!"

"Fun!" the girls whispered back.

Jordan turned to Lola and said, "You're coming, right?"

"Oh, uh —" said Lola.

"Of course she's coming," said Anna.

Lola couldn't believe her luck. The first week of school was over, and she already had a group of cool friends. And now a sleepover party. Lola and her mother went to the mall that night and bought a new sleeping bag. Lola insisted on a backpack, too. She picked out a purple one. It wasn't the same brand the other girls had, but it was the right size. Lola liked the way it felt on her shoulders. She was sure it would help her fit in.

On Saturday night, Lola's dad drove her to Anna's house. "Have fun, honey!" he yelled to her as she ran toward the front door.

The other girls were already there. The party was filled with loud music, laughter, pizza, ice cream, and gossip. The entire night, even as the girls laid out their sleeping bags in the big family room at the back of the house, Jordan and her friends never took off their backpacks. Lola tried keeping hers on, but after a while it became uncomfortable.

In fact, Jordan came up to her during a break in the fun and helped Lola slip it off her shoulders. "It's not the same kind," she said to Lola.

Lola felt like someone had hit her in the stomach. *Those two girls in the hall were right,* she thought, her eyes filling with tears.

"What's wrong?" Kate asked, walking over to them.

These girls don't really like me, thought Lola. *I need to go. I'll just call Dad to come pick me up.*

"Her backpack," Jordan told Kate.

"Is that all?" Kate took Lola's hand. "Don't worry about it," she said. "We can help you find another one. Jordan's the queen of bargain stores, and I'm the queen of key chains!"

Jordan smiled at Lola. "You look good in purple, too," she said.

Lola wiped her eyes and smiled back. "Thanks," she said.

It was nearing midnight and all the girls were dressed for sleep, sitting or lying on their sleeping bags. The purple backpacks were still on their shoulders. Lola felt better. They were all talking and laughing when Anna's mother yelled down the hallway, "Lights out, girls!"

Anna rolled her eyes. "You heard her," she whispered. "Lights out, girls." The rest of them giggled.

With the lights off, the family room was surprisingly dark. As Lola snuggled into her sleeping bag, she heard rustling all around her. The girls were taking off their backpacks. *Finally,* thought Lola. Then it was quiet.

Lola woke up an hour later, needing to use the bathroom. Too much soda. She slipped out of her sleeping bag as quietly as she could and stood up in the dark. The other girls were sleeping. Someone was snoring. Someone else was mumbling in her sleep.

Lola remembered where the bathroom was and walked down the short hallway. On her way back, she snapped off the bathroom light and then stood still. Her eyes needed a few moments adjusting from the bright bathroom to the dark hallway. She didn't want to trip or fall over anyone.

Where was her sleeping bag? She stepped carefully, as if she were walking on the balance beam in gym class. Her foot hit someone's back.

"Oops. Sorry," she said.

Lola's eyes were growing more used to the dark. She could see the five shapes of the sleeping girls. She saw her empty sleeping bag. She looked down at the girl she had bumped into. It was Jordan.

Lola bent down. "Sorry," she whispered again. But Jordan didn't move.

Something about the position of her arms bothered Lola. She didn't know why, but she reached out to the sleeping girl and gently touched her arm.

It was cold. Not freezing cold, but it certainly wasn't giving off any warmth. It felt like plastic.

Lola heard the mumbling again. It came from beyond the circle of sleeping bags.

She spotted a shadow next to the wall. A pile of dark purple. *The backpacks,* Lola thought. That's where the girls had put them. But who was mumbling in her sleep?

Lola watched in terror as one of the backpacks moved. It swayed back and forth. It waddled across the carpet like a penguin. The shoulder straps hung on either side like skinny arms. A thin white line appeared on the front of the backpack. A fold in the purple fabric. A fold that seemed to turn into a smile.

"Don't worry," whispered the backpack. "We'll find one for you, Lola." It was Jordan's voice.

Lola was about to scream when she felt something soft and bumpy brush against her leg. She glanced down and saw more backpacks. The one nearest her leg opened its mouth and Lola could see rows and rows of tiny, sharp teeth.

"We'll help you find a new one. The right one," said the backpack.

The backpack's voice was Lola's voice.

Lola fell onto her sleeping bag. The purple creature shuffled toward her and patted her back. "Yes, yes. A new backpack," it said gently. "She will be a perfect fit."

THE VOICE IN THE BOYS' ROOM

Logan needed a break from after-school band practice. He needed to use the boys' room. But he hated using it when other boys were in there. Logan needed his privacy. Which is why, during the break, he ran down the hallways and found a quiet bathroom far away from the band room.

Ah, nice. The cool, dim room was peaceful. Peaceful as a graveyard, his grandma would say.

It was soothing to his ears after the noisy music practice. A super loud note — *fortissimo!* — blasted from the trombone was still pinging through his brain.

He could still hear it, standing in the boys' room. No, it was something else.

A strange voice. Talking on a cell phone, from one of the stalls.

Great. Someone was in there at the same time! Logan would have to wait until that person left before he could finish his business. He coughed. Then he cleared his throat. Hoping the person heard him and got the message: Hurry up and leave!

But no, the voice kept mumbling and mumbling.

The room was dim. There were no windows. One lightbulb in a wire cage hung from the ceiling. Slowly, Logan bent down and twisted his head to peek under the stalls. He moved carefully. He didn't want to lose his balance so that he'd have to touch the cold cement floor with his bare hands. Gross.

Logan counted the bottoms of three white toilets. No feet.

The kid must be sitting, or standing, on the toilet, talking on the phone, Logan thought.

He stood up and shook his head. He knew practically everyone in the school, but he didn't recognize the voice. The voice was deep, but it wasn't a man's voice. It definitely belonged to a kid. An older kid.

Logan recognized a few words. It wasn't as if he was trying to hear on purpose. He couldn't help it.

. . . mumble . . . underground . . . things . . . mumble . . . grave . . . mumble . . .

Afraid to make a sound, Logan stood completely still.

. . . mumble . . . water . . . mumble . . . water . . . mumble . . . everywhere . . .

He carefully tiptoed out of the boys' room and into the hall. Then he leaned against the wall and let out his breath. Who *was* that? What was he talking about? And would he ever leave the room?

Logan started hopping up and down. This was getting serious. A normal person would have finished their business by now and come out.

He crossed his legs and waited ten more minutes. He knew he should head back to the music room, but he had to go. It was building up inside him like a clogged drain. He was probably already late for the second half of practice anyway.

"Are you kidding me?" Logan cried, throwing up his arms. That was it. He was tired of waiting. Kid or no kid, he was going to use that bathroom. He walked back in. He cleared his throat and fake-sneezed so the speaker would hear him. Logan stood still. The voice had stopped.

He glanced down the row of stalls. The doors were swinging open. But he thought the middle door had been shut before.

As Logan walked past the stalls, he realized no one was there. The doors hung open and no one was sitting inside.

Had the voice come from a vent somewhere? Could it have been someone out in the hall, echoing off the dirty wall tiles?

Logan did what he came to do. Then he stood at the sink and washed his hands.

He heard the voice behind him.

. . . mumble . . . underneath . . . mumble . . . water . . . inside . . .

It was coming from the middle stall. Logan shuffled over to the half-open door. He could see the toilet, the silver pipes, the pile of paper towels, and the stupid graffiti on the walls. Another mumble came from the toilet itself. Logan took a few more steps.

A cell phone floated in the water.

Okay. Some kid had dropped his phone without realizing it, and his friend was still talking on the other end. Weird. It looked like a nice phone. The owner would want it back. *I'll take it to the lost and found,* thought Logan.

Then he thought, *Why me?*

Then he thought, *Okay, it's only water.* Logan stooped down to pick up the lost, mumbling phone.

A hairless hand reached up from inside the toilet and grabbed him.

It started to pull.

THE WORLD'S MOST AWESOME TOOTHPASTE

Jared was not a morning person, but his little brother, Harry, was. Every morning, as the two of them got ready for school, he could hear Harry sing out from his bedroom down the hall:

Morning glory,

Morning lark,

Evening owl

Dim and dark.

This morning, Harry was screeching at the top of his tiny lungs. Jared stuck his fingers in his ears and trudged toward the bathroom. He gazed into the mirror above the sink, trying to focus, but he could barely open his eyes. His hair stuck up like angry feathers.

He turned on the cold water and felt around in the medicine cabinet for the tube of toothpaste. Brushing teeth was his Number Two most un-favorite thing in the world. Number One was waking up.

The toothpaste tube felt strangely full and solid. Jared looked down and saw that it was new. A brand he'd never seen before. He squinted at the bright red and golden letters. THE WORLD'S MOST AWESOME TOOTHPASTE.

It was probably cheaper than the regular brand, and his mom was always trying to save a few more cents.

Jared squeezed some glowing white paste onto the stiff bristles of his toothbrush. He raised the brush and stuck it in his mouth. His eyes popped open.

Wow! The taste was amazing. It was like nothing he'd ever tasted before. No, it was like *everything* he'd ever tasted before. He felt as if he'd just drunk ten sodas in a second. Twenty. *Zing!* Energy pulsed through his body. *Zang!* Lightning bolted through his brain cells.

This *was* the world's most awesome toothpaste.

Jared couldn't stop himself. It was just too good. He kept brushing. The awesomeness kept growing and growing. The toothpaste kept glowing and glowing.

He ignored the big green clock hanging over the toilet. Who cared if he missed the bus? Big deal if he was late for his first-period art class.

Tink!

Jared looked down. One of his teeth had landed in the metal sink. No big deal. It must have been loose anyway. Jared spit out some of the toothpaste, added more to his bristles, and then continued brushing. He noticed that the water in the sink was turning pink. But it didn't stop him. Jared shrugged, closed his eyes, and kept brushing.

He had to. It was awesome!

The bathroom door swung open.

His brother's little blond head edged around the door and he said, "Come on, Jared. You're making us late —"

Harry froze. Then he screamed. And kept screaming.

Jared stared at him. He looked in the mirror again.

Half of his face was missing. He had brushed away the skin until it was shiny, white bone. The sink was full of blood. His tongue was in tatters.

But his smile? It was awesome!

ONE
HUNDRED
WORDS

Nobody believes me. But I still have to tell someone, anyone. You. Whoever is reading this,

PLEASE READ CAREFULLY.

Our brains are falling apart.

Doctors don't know what to call it. Kids call it "Zombie Creep." It started in Iceland. Now it's everywhere. You get it from breathing the same air as a sick person. Your brain gets smaller and smaller. You can tell you have it because it rots your thinking. Your words.

Soon you can only use a few words at a time. Only a hundred each day! But there's a cure. All you have to do is

THE PHANTOM ON THE PHONE

Ella received an odd text on her phone one morning from her friend Hayley.

Who's the girl in your pic???

Ella texted back:

What pic????

Hayley sent a pic with her next text.

This selfie u sent. Who's the girl in the background?

Ella looked closely at her phone. The picture was of her, Ella, making a goofy face at the camera. It was taken in Ella's backyard, full of bright sunshine. *I don't remember this*, thought Ella. In the background, beside the birdfeeder in the middle of the yard, stood a tall, skinny girl.

Ella zoomed in, but the image got fuzzier. It was hard to make out the girl's face, but Ella could tell there was something disturbing about it. She texted Hayley.

Does she have a monkey face?

Hayley replied:

LOL she does!!

It must be a mask, thought Ella. *But who is she?*

Then Hayley sent another photo.

Whats the joke? U just sent this one 2

Ella stared at her phone screen. *What is Hayley talking about?* she wondered. *I didn't send anything.*

The new photo showed the backyard again. Ella was not in the picture this time. The camera shot a view of her back door. The girl was standing there, reaching for the door handle.

Thinking of the back door of their house, which opened directly into the kitchen, Ella shouted from her bedroom. "Mom! Are you in the kitchen?"

Ella didn't get a response. "Mom?" she

called again. No reply, but she heard the back door slam shut.

Her phone chirped — Hayley again.

U r 2 2 funny El

Another photo. This showed the hallway leading to Ella's bedroom. The right side of the pic was fuzzy. It looked like a girl's shoulder.

"Mom?"

There was a creak in the hallway. Ella's house was old, and the uncarpeted floors always creaked and groaned whenever someone walked across them.

Chirp. Another pic from Hayley. This photo showed a close-up of Ella's bedroom door from the outside. A shadow that looked like a hand was reaching for the knob.

Ella had had enough. Why was Hayley pulling this prank on her? And why was Hayley sending her pics that she, Ella, was supposed to be taking? Wouldn't she have already seen those pictures?

Ella tapped Hayley's phone number on her screen and waited. Finally, Hayley came on. "Hey, El, what's up?" she said, brightly.

"Ha, funny, " said Ella. "You know what's up all right."

"What are you talking about?"

"The pictures," said Ella angrily. "Why do you keep texting me and sending me those creepy pictures?"

There was silence from the other end of the line. Then Hayley said, "I haven't been texting you. I'm helping my brother with his homework."

"Then why do you keep sending those —"

"I haven't been sending you anything," said Hayley. Now it was her turn to sound angry. "And I don't even know what pictures you're talking about. Why did you call me up just to yell at me?"

"I'm not yelling at you!" said Ella.

Click! Hayley hung up.

Ella couldn't move. She sat on her bed, warm sunshine spilling across her jeans, and shivered. The knob turned. Slowly, the door pushed open.

"Who's there?" said Ella. The door opened. Her mom stood there, hand on the knob, smiling at her.

"Are you all right?" asked her mom. "You look worried."

Ella gave a little laugh. "I'm fine. I was just texting with Hayley."

"Well, that's good," said her mom. "Because there's a friend here to see you."

"Who?" asked Ella.

"I've never met her before," said her mom. "She said she's in your class."

Ella slowly got up and followed her mother into the kitchen. A cold wave of fear washed over her.

"That's funny," said her mother. "She was right here."

"I have to call Hayley," said Ella. She ran back to her room.

As she flung open the door, she froze. A monkey-headed girl was sitting on her bed.

UNDER COVERS

I love comics.

Especially the old-timey ones like my grandpa collects. Whenever I stay overnight at Grandpa's house, he drags out these big plastic bins from his back room. He calls the room his office, but it's more like a room-sized junk drawer. He plops the bins down, snaps off the plastic lids, and shows me his favorites.

"Here's the first Amazing Spider-Man issue," he says. "And not that guy in the movies. I mean the real deal, the original. See? Here he is, trapped by the Fantastic Four."

"Cool," I say. And it is. The Human Torch, another hero, is flaming across the cover. He's in the Fantastic Four's headquarters, and

Spider-Man is caught inside a big glass tube. This Spider-Man has webs hanging from his arms. Never saw that before!

Each comic book is inside a thin plastic cover that seals at the top. Grandpa says it protects the paper from aging and falling apart. Too bad they couldn't do that with people. If you could do that with people, when Grandpa got older, I could put him inside one and take him out on special occasions.

Grandpa puts the Spider-Man comic back in the bin carefully. He must have hundreds in there. All stacked up like individual slices of plastic-wrapped cheese.

"Aha! Here's one you haven't read before!" Grandpa says. He sounds like he's just discovered buried treasure. "Superman gets trapped in the far future when the sun grows old and turns red!"

That's bad. Everyone knows Superman has no powers under a red sun.

At night, before bed, Grandpa always lets me choose two comics to read by myself. "But you can't lie down. You have to sit up," he orders. "Otherwise, you'll fall asleep and roll over on the comic."

I don't blame him for wanting to be extra careful. Some of those old comics are worth tons of money. I looked up that first Spider-Man issue online. If Grandpa ever sold it, he could get two thousand bucks!

Tonight, I'm right in the middle of my second comic, a Legion of Super-Heroes adventure.

"Ten o'clock, kid," Grandpa yells from the hallway. "Lights out!"

Grandpa is strict about his lights-out rule. Even if I'm in the middle of a comic, I have to turn off the light.

Which is why, for this visit, I brought a mini-flashlight with me.

I flip off the light and wait. I count to one hundred. I figure Grandpa will be in bed by now himself. Yup, I can hear him snoring.

I crawl under the covers and switch on the flashlight. It's perfect. It's like hiding in a tent. I finish the Legion adventure. Element Lad saves his fellow Legionnaires by turning the bad guy's feet into uranium, the heaviest element on Earth!

My eyes are droopy, and it's a little stuffy under the covers. I switch off the light and crawl back toward the pillows. Funny. I can't feel the edge of the sheet above me. So then I crawl what feels like ten feet. The bed itself is only six feet long.

I crawl farther. I still can't find the end. What is going on?

I switch the flashlight back on. I try standing up, but the sheet above me is heavy, like the roof of a tent. I can barely rise up on my knees, pushing against the sheet with my head and reaching out with one arm to make as much space as possible. I swing the light back and forth. No sight of the end of the sheet. No pillows. No bed. I don't see the other comic, either — the first one I had read.

This is crazy. I try a different direction. Maybe I can reach the side of the bed and crawl out.

That doesn't work either. I must crawl for ten whole minutes, and I never reach the end. How can a sheet be this long? What happened to the bed? Where is Grandpa?

"Grandpa!" I yell. No answer. Maybe he can't hear me under this fabric. I yell some more, but I never hear him answer.

So I crawl toward what I think is the foot of the bed. I move as fast as I can. It's hard moving fast on a soft, lumpy bed — even a bed as long and wide as this one seems to be — with a comic in one hand and a flashlight in the other. I put my head down like an angry bull and plow forward as fast as I can. I'll probably crash into the wooden wall at the foot of the bed, but I don't care. Escaping into the fresh air is worth a bruised skull.

No such luck. I crawl and crawl for hours.

The flashlight won't last much longer. The batteries will give out soon.

Then I see it. A light in the distance. The edge of the bed!

As I crawl toward the light, it seems to change. It looks less and less like light peeping under the edge of a sheet and more like a car's headlights down a long dark street. I crawl closer. The beam grows smaller and sharper. Another flashlight!

It's another kid crawling toward *me*.

In his other hand, he holds a comic. Three or four other kids are crawling right behind him.

"Who are you?" he asks.

"What do you mean, 'who are you?'" I say. "What are you guys doing in my bed?"

"Your bed?" comes a muffled voice from behind the flashlight-leader-guy.

The flashlight guy snorts. "You don't get it," he says. "This ain't anybody's bed. I don't know what it is, but it ain't a bed."

"We've been trying to find a way out since last night," says a kid in back.

"Since two nights ago!" says another.

The leader gives me a look. "I don't know how long we've been in here," he says. "All I know is I was reading a comic under the covers with my flashlight —"

"And when you tried to crawl out, this is where you ended up," I say.

He nods.

"I was reading Spider-Man," moans a kid in the back.

"Iron Man, a double issue," says another.

"I'm hungry!" groans a third.

How many kids are here, anyway? I wonder.

The flashlight guy shouts over his shoulder to his followers. "If we stay in one direction we'll have to find a way out." Then he looks at me and says, in a whisper, "It can't go on forever, right?"

"Uh, right," I say, not knowing if I'm right or wrong. But I guess I'll find out soon enough.

So I crawl along with the others, holding out my light.

Before long, we come across an abandoned pile of comics. Old ones. Just like Grandpa has. I mean, these ones are vintage and worth a lot of money. Superman. Batman. Green Lantern. The Hulk.

We all get excited. We reach out to pick up the comics, but the pages crumble.

"Wha—what happened?" asks a kid.

"They were old," says another. "Like they've been here forever."

Everyone's quiet. We're probably all thinking the same thing. Forever is a long time.

"We gotta keep moving," says their leader.

So on we go. Crawling and crawling.

The flashlights are growing dim.

THE ELF'S
LAST TRICK

Nathan heard the scream and smiled. *This is the best prank ever,* he thought.

He had come up with the plan only the day before. It began when his teacher, Mr. Garcia, returned the students' book reports before the final bell. Mr. Garcia weaved in and out of the rows, dropping a report on each desk. At the top of Nathan's report was a C minus scrawled in red, bright as a bug bite. *A C minus?* Nathan thought. *Well, I did write the report in less than twenty minutes, and most of it I copied off the Internet. So what? It still doesn't deserve such a low grade. Teachers are so unfair.*

At the bottom of his report was a note from Mr. Garcia. "Nathan, you can do so much better than this!" Nathan hated when teachers said that. How did they know what he could or couldn't do?

He crumpled up the paper and shoved it in his desk. He hoped no one nearby saw the horrible red grade. Nathan was sure his face was red, too. He looked at Mr. Garcia and glared. What a fake smile the teacher had. *Fake smile.* That's when Nathan remembered the elf. And that's when the plan began forming in his brain.

Nathan's family loved to play pranks. Even the grown-ups got into it. Last winter, Nathan's mom had bought an elf doll as a Christmas decoration. Its thick, puffy body was two feet high, with bendable legs and arms. The oversized head had lobster-red hair tucked under an emerald green cap with a white puffball on top. The face looked real. Hard, bright eyes, rosy cheeks, a wide smile with teeth. Everyone agreed that the doll looked creepy. Which made it perfect for scary tricks.

The first victim had been Nathan. Nathan's dad had hid the elf in his bed. After the boy had gone up to his room, his scream echoed through the house. It was followed by hoots of laughter. The elf showed up more and more in the coming months. More screams. More laughs. More and more pranks. Finally, when the family had grown tired of the elf, and no one jumped or gasped when they saw its eerie smile coming from a closet or refrigerator or washing machine, the creature was stuffed in a box, along with the other holiday decorations, stacked on a shelf in the garage, and forgotten.

But Nathan remembered. Coming home from school, still angry about the unfair grade, he went straight to the garage. He climbed onto a chair, pulled the box from its shelf, snuck the elf into his bedroom, and stuffed it in his backpack. The next day, he walked to school extra early and hid the elf in his locker.

When the last bell rang, Nathan stayed after school in the media center. After a while, he quietly slipped out of the center and hurried to his locker. He stuffed the elf into his backpack again, looking around to make sure no one saw him, and raced down the empty halls toward Mr. Garcia's room.

The door was unlocked. Nathan crept over to Mr. Garcia's desk. He placed the elf on the teacher's chair, and then turned it so the elf was facing away. When Mr. Garcia came in the next morning, he would turn his chair back around and — surprise! The elf would strike again.

Nathan had just stepped outside and closed the door when he heard footsteps. He raced behind the closest row of lockers and flattened himself against the wall. Someone was turning the corner.

Mr. Garcia, Nathan thought. *He must have forgotten something.* Luckily, the teacher didn't see Nathan, and he disappeared through the door to the classroom. Nathan held his breath. This was better than he'd hoped. He had planned for Mr. Garcia to find the elf the next morning before school started, but now . . .

Ah, the terrifying scream!

Nathan smiled. Best prank ever. He stayed hidden a few more minutes. He'd leave as soon as Mr. Garcia came back out and left. But he didn't. Ten, twenty minutes went by, and the teacher still had not come out.

Nathan started sweating. *Sooner or later,* he thought, *another teacher or grown-up will come walking down the hall. They'll ask what I'm doing, and then . . . I'll be caught. I need to get out of here!*

So without a backward glance, Nathan flew down the hall toward the front door. He ran all the way home. His ribs were burning by the time he reached the garage. But he didn't care. It was all worth it. Mr. Garcia would never learn who had left the elf, never know who had given him the fright of his life. *Serves him right,* thought Nathan. *No one gives me a C minus.*

The next morning in Mr. Garcia's room, the students got a surprise. Sitting in their teacher's chair was the school principal, Mrs. Holloway.

"Good morning, class," she began. "I have some bad news, I'm afraid. Mr. Garcia will not finish the rest of the year with us."

Nathan's stomach turned to ice and his thoughts started racing. *Did the shock of seeing the spooky elf make Mr. Garcia sick? Was it his heart? Was he in the hospital?*

Nathan glanced nervously around the room. The elf was nowhere in sight. Someone must have thrown it away.

Mrs. Holloway walked to the door, smiling. She turned to the class. "But don't worry," she said cheerfully. "We were lucky enough to find a substitute." Mrs. Holloway opened the door and called, "Won't you please come in, Ms. Selph?"

A merry little woman stepped into the room. Her curly hair was lobster red. She wore an emerald green sweater with a white puffy collar. Her eyes were shiny and hard. Her cheeks were rosy. And her smile was wide as a shark's.

The chill spread from Nathan's stomach to his chest, his neck, his face.

"Children, Ms. Selph will be your new teacher for the rest of the year," said Mrs. Holloway. "Can we all say 'good morning'?"

"Good morning, Ms. Selph," echoed the class.

Ms. Selph beamed at the students. Her smile, if it was possible, grew even wider.

"Wonderful," she said. Her voice sounded bright as a bell. "I'm so glad to be here. I know it must be quite a surprise to have a new teacher in the middle of the year," she went on. "But not all surprises are bad."

Her shiny eyes blinked, and she looked right at Nathan. "Don't you just love surprises?" she asked.

MICHAEL DAHL TELLS ALL

Can you imagine what a mad scientist's laboratory looks like? You've probably seen one in a movie or video game or comic book. The lab is crammed full of odds and ends, like weird electrical equipment, jars full of squishy stuff, animal skeletons, and ancient books with crumbling pages. I sometimes think of my brain as a laboratory. Mine is packed with memories, riddles, and jokes, voices of people I've met, stories from my family, pictures I've seen in books or museums. And when I start thinking of writing a story, I start picking up odd scraps, bits and pieces here and there. Like a mad scientist, I fit them together into a strange new invention. Here's a list of some of the nuts and bolts that helped build the stories in this book.

SECTION 1: INSIDE THE HOUSE

THE STRANGER ON THE STAIRS

This tale was the result of a challenge I gave myself: What's the creepiest story I can write using the least amount of words?

KNOCK, KNOCK

When I was a kid, my aunt and her five daughters lived in an old house in northern Minnesota that was once a hotel for loggers. It was gigantic and isolated, with a dark, crumbly sauna built underneath. My mom and sisters and I would visit them for several weeks during summer vacations. We spent the evenings telling scary stories and watching *Twilight Zone* reruns.

When I started thinking about scary stories to write, the old loggers' lodge seemed like the perfect setting for a ghost story. I combined that with the truly scary winters we get in Minnesota, where some people have indeed frozen to death while accidentally locked outside their homes.

COLD SEAT

I had just moved into my new house, and I was coming out of the upstairs bathroom one night when I saw Helen — the ghost who lives in my house — for the first time. Since then, I've found bathrooms . . . unsettling. While on the subject of toilets, my friend and fellow writer Donnie Lemke suggested that a warm seat is worse than a cold seat — for the very reason that comes up in the story.

THE LAVA GAME

Do you play the Lava Game? Sometimes my friends and I called it the Poison Game. My mother didn't like the game, whatever it was called, because we bounced all over her good furniture. We never considered quicksand, because that would be too hard to act out. It was easy to pretend you were being burned up by lava or had been poisoned — you simply screamed loudly and then fell over. But how could you sink down into a rug? This story was a way of finding out what might happen.

DON'T LET THE BEDBUG BITE

You can't write scary stories without one of them being about a babysitter. I heard so many creepy tales growing up that involved babysitting — the house is unfamiliar, the grown-ups are gone, it's dark outside. These ingredients set the heart racing. My friend Beth has an amazing kid named Sam who once was afraid of bedbugs. Sam was sure he saw a bug in his bed. If I were Sam, I'd be afraid of bedbugs, too. I wondered, what if the bug wasn't in the bed, but *was* the bed?

THE BACK OF THE CLOSET

Ever since I was five years old and dreamed that a steady stream of bears came lumbering out of my closet toward me, I have not cared much for them. They're dark, stuffy, and things can get easily lost inside them. Closets, I mean, not bears. What if something *worse* than a bear was inside a closet?

HAIKUKU

Making up haiku, a form of Japanese poetry, has been a pastime of mine since I learned what they were in fourth grade. Recently I read a scary haiku by the author Katherine Applegate, creator of Animorphs and *The One and Only Ivan.* She inspired me to make my own spooky mini-tale, in only seventeen syllables.

DON'T MAKE A WISH

There's an old saying: Be careful what you wish for, because it might come true. How bad could a wish be, especially at a fun event like a birthday party? I like to use this formula for scary stories: start with something happy or cheerful, and then see what could possibly go wrong.

SECTION 2: AROUND THE CORNER

MEET THE PARENTS

When we were kids, my sisters and I often imagined that we were adopted. Our real parents, we believed, were rulers of some European kingdom, waiting to reclaim us. Waiting for us to return to a castle, riches, and an endless supply of books and ice cream. Well, what if our true parents were not wonderful, but horrible? Or even monstrous? What would that be like?

CLOSER AND CLOSER

I rode the bus to grade school and high school. Then I rode a bus to college, and then to work. I spent a lot of time on buses observing people, overhearing weird conversations, and staring out the window. Buses don't seem like scary places at all, which made me want to write a story about one. One thing that does creep me out: black plastic garbage bags. They look like slug monsters. Blob creatures. I don't like how the plastic feels either. And who knows what's *really* inside those bags?

LOVE BUG

My friend Donnie strikes again! He and I were chatting about how creepy it would be for humans to turn into centipedes, and — voilà! — the story was born. (Isn't it nice having friends who you can talk to about anything?) As I was writing, I thought it would be even worse if the half-human, half-insect was someone you really liked.

PICKLED

Tornadoes are common in the Midwest. When I was in fifth grade, four of them jumped over my house. My family was lucky. Those same tornadoes ripped apart our town, carved craters in our streets, and damaged many lives. Which is why I still fear storms. I've sat in many basements waiting for storms to pass. But how long should a person wait to come out? I've read about soldiers who hid during World War II and didn't know the war was over until years later. In the dark, it's easy to lose track of time.

DEAD END

I was driving home from work and saw a Dead End sign. *Whoosh!* The whole story jumped into my brain. It probably has something to do with my fear of getting lost. See? I told you that lots of things scare me.

THE DOLL THAT WAVED GOODBYE

One of the most frightening TV shows I ever watched was about a girl whose doll changed places with her. They each took turns being the doll and being the owner. Another spooky story on the show *The Twilight Zone* had a doll that could talk and sneak around the house at night. Both dolls were very protective of their owners. Very. The location of my story was inspired by the many summers I spent as a kid at a camp in northern Minnesota.

HALLOWEEN HEAD

Ordinary objects can become frightening when they appear in places you don't expect them. I was looking at my stash of brown paper grocery bags the other day and asked myself, *Could these be scary? They're so harmless and normal.* Then I wondered, *what if you put something into a bag and then it wasn't there?* I was thinking about all this a few weeks before Halloween. One windy October night all the pieces of the story fit together like the bones of a skeleton. My favorite part of the story: the little eyeholes in the bag.

NIGHT CRAWLERS

The word "night crawler" gives me the creeps. When I heard about a movie that came out with that title, an image flashed through my mind of a human crawling at night through dark, lonely woods. Crawling and crawling. I had to find out where that person came from, so I wrote the story to find out.

CHALK

I saw a young girl holding a stick of chalk, and I immediately thought it was a bone. (I hope it wasn't!) After a few hours at my computer, I had the first draft of the story.

SIDEWALKS FROM OUTER SPACE

When I was in fourth and fifth grade, I had a recurring nightmare about aliens landing in my backyard. My friends and I tried to hide behind trees and bushes, but we were always caught. That's when I woke up, breathing hard and staring out the window to make sure I didn't see fleets of ships hanging in the night sky. I think I was freaked out after watching the 1953 sci-fi movie *Invaders from Mars* on TV. (Here's a weird note: the film's writer was inspired by a dream his wife had about aliens invading the planet. Hmm. What do you call it when different people have the same dream? Creepy!)

SNOW MONSTER

One of my favorite kinds of stories is where you're reading along, minding your own business, and then someone drops a plot twist and — boom! — everything changes. Then you go back and reread the story to find out how you were tricked. Once you know the trick, you can't wait to re-watch the film or reread the book and see how it all fits together. I used the snowy woods as a backdrop because of hunting stories I've heard from friends in Minnesota, Wisconsin, and Iowa.

SECTION 3: OUT OF YOUR MIND

BLINK!

One of my favorite Doctor Who episodes is called "Blink." It's about evil statues that move toward you when you're not looking! I challenged myself to think up a story that would be completely different but would have the same name. Blinking made me think of eyes, and that made me think of eye doctors, and that made me think of eye drops. And drops made me think of elevators. Weird, I know. But that's where stories come from.

A PERFECT FIT

Sleepovers are the perfect time for telling scary stories. What if having a sleepover was the scary story? The story's subject came from my memories of middle and high school. I always disliked cliques, those special little groups where all the members look and act and sound alike. Are they robots, or worse . . . ?

THE VOICE IN THE BOYS' ROOM

Quiet, empty restrooms (for boys or girls) are just plain spooky. Period. This story gives one reason why!

THE WORLD'S MOST AWESOME TOOTHPASTE

You've seen those ads on television that promise amazing results from their super cool products. But who are those people who sell them? And who makes that stuff? It could come from anywhere, right? So what if someone, like a well-meaning mother, ordered a product like that for her kids? Things could go terribly wrong.

ONE HUNDRED WORDS

My friend Donnie gave me a challenge. "What if you only had one hundred words to tell a story?" he asked. "What if something terrible was happening to you, and you only had one hundred words to ask for help?" This short short story was my answer to that challenge.

THE PHANTOM ON THE PHONE

I was brainstorming with my friend Benjamin Bird about the terrifying possibilities surrounding photos on a phone. With some instant phone messaging apps, the pictures disappear after only a few minutes. Ben pointed out that if you saw something bizarre or unusual on one of these pics, you wouldn't always be able to show other people. The evidence could quickly disappear. How would you convince your friends that you were telling the truth about an upsetting photo? You'd be the only one who saw it. And some apps are so easy even a monkey could use them.

UNDER COVERS

I've spent many school nights under the covers with a flashlight and a comic book. I still read comics in bed, though now I'm old enough that I don't need anyone's permission. One night when I was a kid, I had been reading a terrific story about the Legion of Super Heroes, and for some reason I got all turned around under the sheets. It took me a few seconds to realize I was heading in the wrong direction, toward the foot of the bed. But recently, as I thought about those long-ago nights, I wondered what would have happened if I *hadn't* found the way out. Then what? A lot of good stories spring into shape when you simply ask, "What if . . . ?"

THE ELF'S LAST TRICK

The elf is real and has been a member of my family's Christmas tradition for many years. It currently resides in my basement. At least, I *think* it's still down there . . .

ABOUT THE AUTHOR

Michael Dahl, the author of the Library of Doom and Troll Hunters series, is an expert on fear. He is afraid of heights (but he still flies). He is afraid of small, enclosed spaces (but his house is crammed with over 3,000 books). He is afraid of ghosts (but that same house is haunted). He hopes that by writing about fear, he will eventually be able to overcome his own. So far it is not working. But he is afraid to stop. He claims that, if he had to, he would travel to Mount Doom in order to toss in a dangerous piece of jewelry. Even though he is afraid of volcanoes. And jewelry.

ABOUT THE ILLUSTRATOR

Xavier Bonet is an illustrator and comic-book artist who resides in Barcelona. Experienced in 2D illustration, he has worked as an animator and a background artist for several different production companies. He aims to create works full of color, texture, and sensation, using both traditional and digital tools. His work in children's literature is inspired by magic and fantasy as well as his passion for the art.